DOUBLE-
DARE
O'TOOLE

DOUBLE-DARE O'TOOLE

O'TOOLE

CONSTANCE C. GREENE

A Yearling Book

Published by
Dell Publishing Co., Inc.
1 Dag Hammarskjold Plaza
New York, New York 10017

Grateful acknowledgment is made to Shapiro, Bernstein & Co.
Inc. for permission to reprint two lines from the song "I
Double Dare You" by Terry Shand and Jimmy Eaton. Copyright MCMXXXVII, Renewed by Shapiro, Bernstein & Co.
Inc. All rights reserved.

Yearling ® TM 913705, Dell Publishing Co., Inc.

ISBN: 0-440-41982-4

Reprinted by arrangement with The Viking Press
Printed in the United States of America

Seventh Dell printing—June 1985

To Ed Mulford,
who gave me the idea

DOUBLE-DARE O'TOOLE

1

FEX O'TOOLE CASED THE HALL, LOOKING BOTH WAYS as if he were preparing to cross a busy street. The coast was clear. It was recess and the school was empty except for him and the six or seven guys behind him, egging him on.

"How'd I get roped into this, anyway?" he asked, angrily and too late.

"Go on, Fex! Slip in there! Lay it on him!" The voices hissed in unison, sounding like air being let out of a bunch of tires. "Sock it to him, Fex baby!" He felt a hand in the middle of his back, urging him forward.

"Quit it," he said, turning. "This is stupid. I don't want to do it. What's the point?"

"Hey." Barney Barnes, the leader and, sad to say, the brains of the outfit, raised his eyebrows in astonishment. His long, flat face looked as if it had been pasted on top of his short neck, giving him the appearance of a badly made puppet. "He don't want to do it. Whadya think about that?" All the faces assumed astonished looks. They'd never heard anything so amazing in all their lives.

Then a voice, gentler than the rest, said, "I double-dare you, O'Toole. I double-dare you," it said a second time. For good measure. The words came out slowly, sweetly, like honey oozing from a jar. Without turning, Fex knew whose voice it was. It belonged to a girl he hated. She sat a couple of seats ahead of him in social studies. She had a pointy chin and a pointy nose and wore her white-blond hair in a pony tail. Every time Fex walked down the aisle to the blackboard or anyplace else, she stuck out her foot and tripped him. Her eyes were very pale blue, the palest eyes he'd ever seen.

This girl passed a lot of notes. She was an expert at passing notes without getting caught. Back and forth across the seats she passed her many-folded squares of paper to people she hardly knew. Once she'd sent a note to Fex. It said, "Fexy is sexy."

As he opened it, he refused to look in her direction, although he could feel her watching him. He'd torn the note into many tiny pieces and made a big show of piling them up in a heap.

Was it true? Was he sexy?

Fex walked rapidly to the door of the principal's office, tapped lightly, and waited. As he'd expected, there was no answer. He turned the knob. The door wasn't locked. That meant Mr. Palinkas was out to lunch and his secretary was down in the teachers' room getting coffee to drink with her yogurt. She'd be back any minute. The timing was right.

He opened the door and peered inside, hoping some stranger would ask, "May I help you?" In the principal's office they said, "May I help you?" rather than "Can I help you?" A very small but important difference.

He could always make an excuse, say he was looking for Mr. Palinkas and he'd come back later. Sun lay in heavy bands on the floor. Three withered daffodils sat in a glass of water, breathing their last. The Venetian blinds were crooked, the windows needed washing. Mr. Palinkas' desk was neat and tidy, the yellow pencils and the fat red erasers lined up like little soldiers. From the playground Fex could hear shouts and other sounds of enjoyment. He wished he were out there instead of in here.

Out of the corner of his eye he saw the mob swelling up behind him, whispering and jostling one another, acting as if it were Saturday afternoon and they were standing in line to get into the movies.

Barney smiled at Fex, encouraging him. "You're doing great," he said.

Fex took the piece of paper out of his pocket, unfolded it, and laid it in the middle of the blotter where it couldn't be missed. He kept his head turned because he didn't want to look at the crude drawing of a large, ugly pink pig and the caption, which said, "Your a pig, Palinkas." As an afterthought, the inspired artist had drawn a large hand, the middle finger extended, beside the pig's nose.

"Jerks don't even know how to spell," Fex muttered. There was the sound of scuffling down the hall. Barney stuck his head around the corner.

"Way to go," he cheered Fex on. Barney, by reason of being the biggest, strongest, oldest kid in the sixth grade, was the one who laid down the ground rules. He'd repeated kindergarten and first grade and was a natural bully.

"Why pull a stupid stunt like this anyway?" Fex had said. "Palinkas isn't that bad."

"Hey." Barney's eyebrows had shot up and out of sight underneath his hair. "Hey, he's the principal, right?" as if that said it all.

Fex shuddered. Somebody just walked over my grave, he thought. He walked out of the office, past the milling throng, and, almost running, made the stairs just as Mrs. Timmons, the secretary, was coming up, clutching her paper cups of coffee and yogurt.

"Hello, Fex," she said. "How come you're inside on a beautiful day like this?" She liked him because last winter he'd helped her push her car out of a snowdrift.

He gave her a small salute with his hand. "I'm on my way out right now," he said. "See you."

He had time for one turn at bat and hit a perfect line drive. It was a beauty, so straight and fast that no one could've caught it. If the bell hadn't rung right at the crucial moment, it would've been a home run for sure. On an ordinary day that would've made him feel great. But today wasn't an ordinary day. He tramped back inside, keeping his head down.

There's nothing worse than knowing you've been a fool and have no one to blame but yourself. That was the worst of it. When you know better and behave like an ass anyway.

2

ON HIS WAY HOME FEX CUT THROUGH SODERSTROMS'
yard, hoping their German shepherd was chained and
sleeping off his dinner. All was quiet. God was with him.
The long grass waved its green tentacles at him, imitating
an octopus. Mr. Soderstrom was, as usual, a week behind
in his mowing.

Charlie Soderstrom scaled the sides of his sandbox,
making guttural noises to indicate his troops were lined up
against his dinosaurs and the dinosaurs were probably
winning.

"How's it going, Charlie?" Fex said.

Charlie stood up. His stomach peeped out from between

his cowboy shirt and his jeans like a little face with only one eye, smack in its middle. He jabbed his thumb down at the bodies of his fallen soldiers.

"They got the flu," he said. Charlie always made excuses for them. "They're throwing up all over my monsters." Charlie was four. His mouth was very red, and curled up at either end when he was happy. Now it had turned itself down at the corners, getting ready for trouble. His cheeks were round with baby fat.

"Tough," Fex said. "Try a shot of ginger ale. It's very good for flu."

Charlie nodded, cheered up immediately, and trotted inside for a shot of ginger ale. His mother left him a lot with sitters when she went shopping or to bridge luncheons. He was good at playing by himself. Sometimes Fex baby-sat when the Soderstroms went out. They paid him. He would've done it for nothing.

Fex crossed the single-plank bridge that spanned the stream, peering down into the bright water. No fish today. They smelled him coming, he was sure, and passed the word along. Then each fish hid behind its own special rock, thumbing its nose (if fish had noses) at him.

Up ahead he saw the outlines of the house, snuggled against the side of the hill. When he got there, he squashed his nose against the window to see inside.

The woman there, bending over, looked up, startled. When she saw him, she dropped the bundle of clothes she was carrying.

"You! Francis!" she hollered. "Stop spying on me!"

The spell broken, he hotfooted it for freedom. But the woman was fleet of foot and long of arm. Even after she grabbed him, Fex's legs continued to churn, his muscles straining against captivity.

"Hey, Mom," he said, "it's only me. Your son, Francis Xavier. What's the matter, can't you take a joke?"

Somewhat reluctantly, she released him. He rubbed his ear, hoping it was still in working order.

"One of these days, Fex," she said, "you'll go too far. You'll pull that trick on someone and they'll think you're an escaped convict and call the police, and from then on it'll be curtains," and she drew her finger across her throat and made a gurgling sound which he fully understood.

"As long as you're here, help me pick up this stuff." They bent and made a big pile of blue jeans, shirts, and underwear. Fex's clothing was marked with red tape, Pete's with blue, and Jerry's yellow. His mother was taking a business management course in adult education and applying things she learned there to her home.

After her first lesson the tempo of living in the O'Toole household had picked up considerably. "The secret is," Mrs. O'Toole told anyone within range, "do not waste a moment. Time is money, as we all know. Every minute counts."

Last year a course in nutrition had commanded her attention. With it came hot cereal, no junk foods, no sugar, whole wheat bread. She stood over them with her arms crossed on her chest, watching them like a prison warden as they shoveled down their throats the goodies she'd decided they should consume.

"Your brain works better if you have a nice hot breakfast," she told them. "None of that sugar-coated, packaged junk for my family." She had become a fanatic on the subject. For snacks they ate saltines. Once, in a sugarless-induced frenzy, Fex had driven an ice pick through the top of a can of mandarin oranges and had drunk the juice like a man straight out of the desert.

No amount of protesting did any good. The only one in the family who escaped was Mr. O'Toole.

"How come Dad doesn't get any?" Fex had asked, noting the jaunty manner in which his father hid behind his newspaper and managed to snag his cup of coffee without revealing himself. It was as if there were nothing behind the paper but a disembodied hand.

"I think Dad needs hot cereal more than we do. We all count on Dad. Where would we be without him?" Fex warmed to his subject. "He brings home the bacon, doesn't he? You should pay more attention to what he eats, Mom."

Dad rattled his paper and stayed hidden. And avoided the hot cereal treatment.

Now Fex and his mother carried the clean clothes up the cellar stairs and into the kitchen.

"How was your day, darling?" She sometimes called him darling when they were alone.

"Lousy," he said. "Absolutely lousy."

"That bad? What happened?"

He shrugged. "Nothing I can put my finger on. I'll take the laundry upstairs," and he grabbed a bundle and climbed the stairs two at a time, before she had a chance to question him further.

After he'd gotten rid of the piles of clean clothes, Fex fell back on his bed and stared at the underside of Jerry's bunk.

Gimme a break, he thought, one crummy break. Not two or even three. One. To see me through.

Through what? He began to kick the wall, as if he were getting even. He concentrated on one fat clown face on the wallpaper that had always irritated him. The clown stopped smiling in that ridiculous way, and Fex felt a small stab of pleasure which increased when he saw that the plaster behind the clown's sad face had begun to crumble. Good. Fex kicked a couple more times, for good measure.

He heard the sound of feet running up the stairs and hastily got up. Whoever it was, he didn't want to be caught lying down in the middle of the day.

"Your mother said you were up here," Audrey said. She stood in the doorway. "You want to come over? I've got some new records."

Audrey lived two blocks away on Perry Avenue. She had short, crisp black hair, very dark eyes, and narrow arms and legs. Her eyebrows, Fex thought, looked as if someone had taken a black crayon and drawn a straight line over each of her eyes. She was two months older than Fex and, he suspected, much smarter than he. They'd been friends since kindergarten.

"Nah." Fex opened his bureau drawer and rummaged through it as if he expected to find buried treasure in its depths. "I got stuff to do."

Audrey crossed her arms and leaned against the door.

"Fex," she said.

"What?" he snarled.

The room seethed with her silence. "Nothing," she said and thundered down the stairs. He heard the front door slam.

That'd bring out his mother, wanting to know what was what. His mother liked to keep her finger on the pulse.

He waited. In a few minutes she called, "Want some cocoa?"

"No," he shouted. "Thanks anyway." He lay down again and picked at the hole in the plaster, enlarging it.

"I don't want any lousy old cocoa," he whispered. "You

know what you can do with your lousy old cocoa."

But what good was it to assert yourself, play tough, when there was no one to hear you? He got up, went into Pete's room, and checked all the usual hiding places. No *Playboy* there. Pete must've taken it to school to show the center-fold. That was some centerfold. Either that or the old man had latched on to it. Fex had thought his father was too old for that kind of stuff. Pete said nuts to that, you're never too old.

Pete thought he knew everything.

Here I am, Fex thought, almost twelve. I'll be twelve next month. Big deal. He thought about the piece of paper on Mr. Palinkas' desk. I don't know anything.

3

MRS. O'TOOLE PULLED ON HER GLOVES. "WE'LL ONLY be at the Warrens'," she said.

Fex looked at her, then lowered his eyes. "I thought you and Dad were headed for the Academy Awards dinner," he said.

"I'm not overdressed, am I?" she said, looking at herself in the hall mirror.

"You look great, Mom," Jerry said.

Although she hadn't yet left the house, Fex thought his mother already looked like a different person. In her party clothes she shimmered and glowed and seemed covered with a shiny glaze, like a strawberry tart. He felt a trifle shy in her presence. And, although he greatly admired her appearance, he longed for the morning when she'd be herself again.

Mr. O'Toole jingled the car keys.

"You kids behave yourselves," he said, eager to get going.

"Don't call us unless it's an emergency." Their mother pressed her cheek against each of theirs, careful not to smear her lipstick.

"Tell Pete to keep hands off," Jerry said. "When you go out and leave him in charge, he always acts like King Kong."

"Just as long as he doesn't try to climb the Empire State Building," Mr. O'Toole said. He jingled his keys some more.

"No one's in charge," he said. "You're all old enough to look after yourselves."

Fex and Jerry looked at each other. That was a lot of baloney, and they both knew it.

"Be good boys, please," their mother said, and she and their father took off. Fex and Jerry knelt on the sofa and watched the red taillights disappear as the car turned the corner on its way to the Warrens'.

Pete did his usual Dr. Jekyll-Mr. Hyde routine. The minute their parents left, he turned into a monster. Without even drinking a potion.

"All right, you guys," he snapped. "Shape-up time." He whipped out his pad and pencil to take notes on what they did wrong. "Keep your noses clean or else."

Pete was a fifteen-year-old hotshot, Fex thought, the worst kind. He was a sophomore in high school. Girls had been calling him up since he was younger than Fex was now. He was a good athlete, a good student. He was full of himself. When Audrey went to visit her uncle, she sent Fex a postcard. It said, "I used to think nothing was impossible until I met you." That was Pete in a nutshell.

Jerry did what he always did. He took his violin out of its case and tucked it under his chin.

"Not here!" Pete shouted, covering his ears. "Mercy! Have mercy!" Jerry was ten, with the face of a choir boy. Ladies were always patting his cheek, smoothing his hair, driving him bananas. Mostly Jerry was cool and calm. Nothing bothered him. Fex envied him. Jerry got free violin lessons in school. They had to rent the violin, but the lessons were free.

"God knows they ought to be," their father said after he heard Jerry play. Jerry produced the most extraordinary sounds from that violin that Fex had ever heard. Sometimes the house was filled with the mournful sound of a coyote caught in a steel trap. Other times you'd swear someone was locked in a dungeon in the cellar being tortured by experts. Through it all, Jerry smiled as he sawed away. He loved his violin. It was a pleasure to watch, if not listen to him.

Fex figured Jerry didn't hear the same noises his listeners did. Probably to his own ears he sounded like Heifetz. Like most people, he heard what he wanted to hear.

Jerry went upstairs to practice. The telephone rang. It was Sally, for Pete. When the calls first started, Fex listened in on the upstairs extension, hoping to hear some sexy stuff. Pete said, "No kidding!" a lot, and whoever the girl was, she giggled in time to the music in the background. Fex had almost fallen asleep.

Now he rarely bothered to eavesdrop. It wasn't worth it.

Fex lay on the floor, studying his history. His teacher, Ms. Arnow, was always telling him he'd have to concentrate harder if he wanted better marks. Look at me now, Ms. Arnow, he directed. He felt like calling her up and asking her to drop over so she could watch how hard he was concentrating.

He felt the pressure of a foot on his rear end. Just the toe of the shoe, but enough.

"Fexy," his brother Pete said, "I got the urge for some cookies. All that talking made me hungry." Pete spoke in an absentminded way that meant he'd had cookies in mind for some time.

Fex rolled over on his side.

"That Sally you were talking to. She the one on the wrestling team?"

The pressure of Pete's shoe increased. "Ha-ha," he said. "That's about as funny as a fart in a space suit." Fex made earmuffs of his hands and concentrated harder. He knew he should go upstairs to the room he and Jerry shared, but he couldn't fight the violin tonight.

Take a gander, Ms. Arnow. Just a little gander at me, Fex O'Toole, concentrating my butt off.

Bending down so Fex could smell the peanut butter on his breath, Pete whispered, "When you gonna do what I say, kid?"

The blood pounding in his head, Fex told himself, I won't. He can't make me.

"Go get 'em yourself," he said.

"Hate to do this to you, kid," Pete said, "but I don't have a choice. *I double-dare you.*"

Jerry straggled through the living room on his way to the kitchen for a snack. They ate more snacks when their parents were out than when they were home. Jerry watched them, waiting.

"Go soak your head," Fex said.

Pete laughed and lay back on the couch. He took off his shoes and socks and picked his toenails, watching Fex out of the corner of his eye.

"A double-dare is a double-dare, baby. You can't escape a first-class double-dare, and you know it."

"Dad would be mad if he heard you," Jerry said.

Fex went on reading. Pete picked a nail off his big toe and threw it at him.

"I double-dare you to sit over here, I double-dare you to lend me your ear," Pete sang, his favorite golden oldie. He'd been delighted to find the record in a secondhand junk shop. Had learned all the words, in fact, and relished every chance he had to break into song for Fex's benefit.

"Don't do it, Fex," Jerry said, his face stern, his eyes glistening. "Hang on and don't give in." He went back upstairs.

I won't, he can't make me, Fex told himself again. Then, as if someone had pulled some strings, as if he were a robot and had no control over his actions, Fex got up, went to the kitchen, grabbed a handful of cookies, kept three for himself as a gesture of independence, and threw the rest in Pete's direction. Pete grinned, picked up the cookies, and didn't even say, "Thanks."

The telephone rang again. Pete arranged his face in what he thought of as his sexy look, letting his lids stall at half mast, curving his hand around the receiver as if he owned it.

"Hello," he said in his deep, mysterious voice. Then, "Who?" he snapped.

"It's for you, creep." He held out the telephone to Fex. "Hurry up. You got work to do."

Not too many people called Fex. Maybe it was Audrey.

"Hello," Fex said.

"I'm taking a survey. I'd like to know if your refrigerator is running." It was Barney's voice. Fex couldn't believe Barney was working that old routine.

"Why, are you trying to catch it?" he replied.

Silence from the other end. Barney breathed into the telephone, trying to think of what to say next.

"Listen. Don't bug me," Fex said. "I know it's you, Barney. I've had a bellyful of you today."

"How'd you know it was me?" Barney said.

"I can smell you," Fex said.

"Ha-ha-ha," Barney answered.

"Listen, my old man's on the warpath. He says no phone calls until my marks improve," Fex said. "I've gotta go. If he catches me, he'll let me have it. He'll probably let you have it too."

"He better not!" Barney hollered. "He just better not."

"Gotta go, Barney," Fex said and hung up.

Upstairs all was quiet. Fex sneaked into his room. Maybe Jerry had gone to sleep with the light on. He pulled on the striped T-shirt he slept in and turned back his blanket.

"Hey!" Jerry hung upside down, like a bat, from his upper bunk.

"I thought you were asleep."

"I was thinking," Jerry said.

"What about?"

"I was thinking you're a jerk to let him get away with that junk."

"What junk?"

"That cookie junk. You oughta punch him out when he tries that stuff."

Fex shrugged. He was a master shrugger. "It doesn't matter."

Jerry scowled. Even scowling he looked angelic. "Sure it matters, and you know it." His upside-down face disappeared. "Listen to this," he commanded as he began a new melody.

Fex listened, wincing.

"Has it got a name?" he asked when the music ended.

Jerry's face dipped over the side at him. "Isn't it neat? That's 'Turkey in the Straw.' That's for square dancing. Do-si-do and all that rot. Maybe they'll ask me to play if they have another square dance at school. I might have to do a solo." The strains of "Turkey in the Straw" fought their way from the violin. Kicking and screaming, Fex thought.

"Some turkey," he said, but Jerry didn't hear him above the sounds of his music.

4

"FEX," MRS. TIMMONS SAID NERVOUSLY, "MR. PALINKAS would like to see you." She'd been waiting in the hall for him. "Right away. In his office." Mrs. Timmons spoke in short sentences when she was agitated.

"O.K." He knew what was coming. His stomach churned, formed several hard little knots. He whistled as he went down the hall. What else could he do?

He knocked and heard Mr. Palinkas say, "Come in, come in," in an impatient voice.

Oh, man. Fex felt a sudden need to go to the bathroom.

I didn't do anything so terrible, he told himself. They can't send me to jail for what I did.

Once he was inside, Mr. Palinkas kept him waiting.

Then, when he was good and ready, he tossed the drawing of the pig at Fex.

"This your work?" he said.

Fex looked at the pig, scowling, as if he'd never seen it before.

"You responsible for this?"

"Responsible?" That was a word he'd noticed grown-ups threw around a lot.

"Yeah, responsible." Mr. Palinkas picked up his walking stick from the chair. He pointed it at Fex. "You have heard the word? You know what it means?" As he spoke he drummed rhythmically against his leg with the stick. Thwack, thwack, it went. That stick was a barometer of Mr. Palinkas' emotions, Fex thought. He'd never seen the principal without it, although he wasn't lame and had no need to carry a walking stick. Fex had heard that when old Palinkas picked up his stick, you better watch out. He had never touched anyone with it, but there had to be a first time, Fex figured.

"You put it there, did you not?" Mr. Palinkas turned his chair sideways, crossed his legs, and looked at his shoes.

Fex nodded. He felt it would be unfair, cowardly even, to defend himself. He had put the drawing on the desk. That couldn't be denied.

"Was there any particular reason for doing such a thing?"

"No, sir." How to explain to this man that Fex O'Toole would do anything and everything he was double-dared to do? How to tell him that without sounding like a first-class wimpy fool?

"I'm sorry," Fex said.

Mr. Palinkas laced his fingers together.

"Do you think that makes it all right? To say you're sorry?"

"No, sir."

"You have something against me?"

Fex shook his head. For no reason, he suddenly remembered the time he'd seen Mr. Palinkas in the supermarket, gazing down into the frozen food, probably deciding what he'd have for dinner. Fex had been in the store buying a box of noodles for his mother. He'd been so startled, so unnerved by seeing the principal in such an unlikely place, performing such a commonplace task, by seeing him someplace other than behind his desk or walking around the halls, thwacking his stick as he went, that he'd turned away, pretending he hadn't seen Mr. Palinkas. What would he say if they should meet face to face in Aisle 2, bending over boxes of sugar, checking the prices?

So he'd skulked around the aisles, waiting for Mr. Palinkas to leave before he did.

Then, when he'd thought the coast was clear, he'd

brought the noodles to the checkout counter, and there was Mr. Palinkas, paying for a package of frozen stuffed peppers.

Frozen stuffed peppers. Imagine Mr. Palinkas buying such a thing. Fex had been amazed. Then, just as the girl handed over the change and threw the peppers into a brown paper bag, Mr. Palinkas had turned, looked Fex in the face, raised his cane in salute, and walked out of the store.

He knew I was there all along, Fex had thought then. He knew.

Now he said, "No, sir, I don't have anything against you."

Mr. Palinkas came around to the front of his desk, carrying his stick. If he hits me, Fex thought, I won't holler. I've got it coming. Even if he raises welts on me, I won't holler. He waited for the blows to fall. Nothing happened.

"Then why?" Mr. Palinkas poked the stick at Fex as he paced back and forth. "You know something? I pride myself on my judgment. I hate to be wrong, especially about kids. I had you pegged for a good one. I figured you had your head on straight, as they say these days. I guess I was wrong." He raised the stick. Here it comes, Fex thought. Mr. Palinkas traced a circle in the air with the stick.

"You have any problems?" he asked.

"No, sir," Fex answered, startled. He hadn't expected that.

"Parents divorced? Stepmother or father you don't get on with? Nothing like that?"

I can't just keep on saying, "No, sir," Fex thought. I sound like a jerk.

"No, sir," he said.

"Your marks all right?"

"They're O.K., I guess."

"Well, then." Mr. Palinkas walked back and sat down at his desk. "If everything's all right at home, no trouble there, no trouble with the marks, what's the answer?" He and Fex looked at each other.

"In this business," Mr. Palinkas said, leaning back in his chair, "you look for problems. You try to find out what's bothering a kid, what makes him do things he shouldn't. You figure maybe a kid's trying to tell you something. Maybe you can do something to help. But everything's all right, is it?"

Fex said, "Yes, sir."

"You know . . ." Mr. Palinkas ran his fingers through his thick gray hair, took out his handkerchief and blew his nose, taking his time.

My gosh, Fex thought, I'm never going to get out of here.

"When I was your age," the principal continued, "the

country was in a terrible depression. My father lost his job at the tile factory and had to pick up us kids and my mother and take us clear across the country to stay with his parents. He not only lost his job, he lost his pride as well." He cleared his throat.

"Maybe you kids have it too soft. Nobody to think about but yourselves. Maybe life's too easy. Not enough travail. Not enough challenge."

Mr. Palinkas sighed. He reached over, took the three withered daffodils out of the glass, and threw them into the wastebasket.

"Mrs. Timmons," he called, "would you mind coming in here for a minute?"

Mrs. Timmons came to the door of the little room where she worked. She had fitted her face with a faint smile of encouragement for Fex. She wore a pale green blouse that matched her eyes. A long yellow pencil was stuck into her hair, over her ear.

"Mrs. Timmons," Mr. Palinkas said, "this young man is available for after-school jobs. For a week, starting tomorrow so he can let his mother know he'll be late. If there's anything that needs doing—mimeographing, supplies to be brought up from the storeroom, wastebaskets to be emptied, Fex will oblige. Perhaps you'd better make a list of things you think he might be able to help you with."

"Yes, Mr. Palinkas," Mrs. Timmons said.

She went back into her little room and shut the door. Fex felt as if he were nailed to the floor.

"Can I . . ." he started to say.

"You're not a mean kid," Mr. Palinkas said. "I'm pretty sure of that. I know all the mean kids. Meanness is hard to hide. But that was a mean thing you did." He gave a long sigh and ran his finger around inside his shirt collar, as if it were too tight for him.

Fex backed toward the door. If he didn't get to the bathroom soon, something terrible might happen.

Mr Palinkas swiveled his chair around so he faced the dirty windows.

"You can go now," he said.

5

AFTER SCHOOL AUDREY WAS WAITING. FEX HAD HALF hoped she would be, half hoped she wouldn't.

"What'd he say?" she asked. Up ahead, Barney Barnes took potshots at a squirrel with his slingshot.

"Who?"

"I can't stand it." Audrey stuffed her hands in her pockets and stalked beside him, her legs as stiff as an angry dog's.

"If you don't want to tell me, say so. But don't pretend you don't know what I'm talking about. That really gets me when you do that. You figure if you don't talk about it, it never happened. Sweet little Francis Xavier O'Toole.

Butter wouldn't melt in your mouth." When Audrey was mad, she didn't fool around.

"We had a talk," Fex said in a monotone. "He wanted to know if I had problems at home. I said no. He said I wasn't mean. He told me to work after school helping Mrs. Timmons for a week, starting tomorrow. That's about it."

Audrey jerked her chin at him as if she were illustrating a point on the blackboard.

"So you didn't tell him about the double-dare bit, huh? You didn't tell him about that moron." She jerked her chin in Barney's direction. "If Mr. Palinkas knew you let that moron egg you into doing some of the things you do, he'd think you were a lunatic."

"How do you know I'm not?" Fex said angrily.

Barney bounced toward them on the balls of his feet. He seemed to know he was being talked about.

"Hey, Fexy," he called. Barney chose to ignore girls. His eyes slid over them as if they weren't there. One thing about Audrey. She was pretty tough to ignore.

"Hey, Fexy," Barney repeated, "got any plans for anything bizarre today?"

"What's 'bizarre' mean?" Audrey asked.

Barney forgot himself and looked at her. "How do I know?" he said.

Girls made Barney nervous. When he was nervous, he

bit his fingernails. With his forefinger he began to explore the back of his mouth.

"You better be careful," Audrey said. "You might chew that down to the knuckle if you don't watch out."

Barney snatched his finger from his mouth.

"If you don't know what 'bizarre' means," she went on, "then how do you know what you're talking about?"

"Let's split," Barney growled to Fex. "Let's you and me split."

"Can't," Fex said. "I've got to go home and tell my mother I'm staying after school for a week. Palinkas found out I put the pig on his desk."

"How'd he find out?" Barney's voice was surly.

"What difference does it make how? He did. That's what counts. What'd he ever do to you anyway? That's what I can't figure."

"You like him!" Barney hooted. "You *like* him! Hey, he's the boss, man. You can't like the boss."

"Who says?"

"You can't, that's all."

"That's dumb," Audrey said.

"Tell her to shut up," Barney said to Fex.

"Tell me yourself."

Barney aimed his empty slingshot at Audrey's feet.

"What'd he do, Barney?" Fex asked.

"He left me back," Barney mumbled. "Twice."

"That's wasn't his fault. He's fair. He listens to your side of the story," said Fex, who hadn't told his side.

"You tell him anything?" Barney asked.

"No. He asked me if I had anything against him and I said no. I said I was sorry and he asked me if I thought that made it all right. So I said no again."

The three of them stood swinging their arms, avoiding each other's eyes.

"Let's go," Audrey said.

"I'm getting a Moped," Barney told Fex.

"Yeah?"

"My mother's boyfriend's in the business. He can get me one at half price. So I'm getting the most expensive kind," Barney bragged.

"Wow." Audrey's eyes went round as quarters. "You're sure you're up for the most expensive kind? I understand there's a big black market in Mopeds these days. Especially the expensive ones." Audrey looked at Barney, smiled at him for the first time. "You'll have to pick the thing up and carry it around with you when you're not on it, Barney. Carry it on your back if you want to make sure nobody rips it off." She went on smiling.

"Why doesn't she shut up?" Barney asked Fex. Fists clenched, he began to bounce around in a circle, taking punches at the air. With each punch, he came closer to Audrey.

Audrey stood her ground, watching him, a faint smile on her lips. Finally she said, "I've got stuff to do, Fex. See you," and she tucked in her elbows and jogged off down the street.

Fex watched her go. "Why do you hang out with her?" Barney asked angrily. "Stuck-up, la-di-da girl like her. I don't get it."

"We're friends."

Barney's face turned crafty, his eyes slits. "She putting out?" he asked, chewing on his finger, smiling at Fex around it. "You getting any?"

Fex backed off. "Don't be a jerk," he said. "I have to split."

"If you want, I can ask my mother's boyfriend if he can get you a Moped half price too!" Barney called. Fex broke into a run, pretending he hadn't heard. As he ran, he thought, I'll go by the store, see if Angie's there. Angie had a way with words. She made him laugh. He felt in need of a few laughs.

6

"ANOTHER DAY, ANOTHER DOLLAR," ANGIE SAID, PEER-ing out from behind a rickety rack laden with small sacks of potato chips. Behind her hung a picture of her son dressed in his army uniform. Under the enormous hat his dark eyes stared out accusingly, his little sloping chin almost swallowed up by his uniform. A small, limp American flag adorned one side of the picture. On the other a pair of gilded baby booties kept watch.

"Just in time." Angie dangled a slightly used tea bag in front of Fex. "This one's been around the track once or twice, but there's life in it yet." She whipped out a tissue from a box she kept handy and wiped off the counter.

"You want cream?" Angie slid a fat chipped cup banded

with blue over to him. "Well, not real cream. Half and half."

Fex knew Angie's half and half. Always on the verge of turning sour, it formed little oily pools on the surface of the tea.

"No, thanks," he said.

"Cracker?" She held out a box. "No sugar in these. You only got one set of teeth. If you don't watch 'em, who will?"

"My mother," Fex said.

Angie tapped her own teeth with a fingernail wearing traces of bright red polish. "Gold, pure gold, worth a fortune," she said, laughing. "A burglar breaks into my house, he heads straight for my teeth. I got all my money in my mouth."

Fex drank his tea and studied Angie from behind his cup. She'd taken off her glasses and was rubbing the red spot they'd left on the bridge of her nose. Without them, he thought, her face looked naked. There were dark purple circles under her eyes. Today, as on all other days, she wore her black sweater and old khakis, which she'd cut down from her son's old army pants.

Suddenly she ducked her head at Fex.

"I'm thinking of dying my hair," she said. "Whadya think? Blond or red? My husband says he'll send me back if I do. Too bad for him. Look at that," she commanded. "Gray hairs. Lots of 'em. How can I keep up with the young chicks with that kinda junk?" She straightened up and put her glasses back on.

"I like you the way you are," Fex said, unexpectedly shy. To his relief, a man came in and asked for his usual.

Angie handed over a pack of cigarettes. "You know what they call these things, Ed? Coffin nails, that's what."

"How about some matches, Ange?" Ed slapped down his money. "You been telling me that for years, kid. Look at me. Strong as an ox." He thumped his chest vigorously and coughed in an exaggerated way.

"You got a nice wife, nice kids," she warned. "You oughta quit."

Ed pocketed the cigarettes. "Maybe next week, Angie. I'm cutting down. That's why I smoke this brand. They taste like old socks. See you around, kid," and he left.

Angie shook her head. "What people do to their bodies. Now take me. Bacon is my downfall. I love bacon. Makes the old cholesterol count go sky-high, right? Do I give it up? Not on a bet. I love bacon. In this life, Fex, you got to have discipline. My mother told me that and, believe me, I'm still looking for it."

Fex's thoughts were elsewhere. "Yeah," he agreed. Then he decided not to beat around the bush.

"Angie," he said. "I have this friend. He's got a problem."

"There's very few folks wandering around out there,"

Angie said, "don't have at least one. What's your friend's problem?"

"Well, he's got this thing about taking a double-dare," Fex said. "Every time somebody double-dares him to do something, he does it, no matter what." Fex frowned down into his empty cup. "He doesn't want to and he knows he's a jerk, but he can't stop. He doesn't know what to do to make himself stop."

"That's a tough one," Angie said. "Let me think."

A little kid came in and marched importantly to the rear of the store. He brought back a bottle of milk and, with the air of a stockbroker involved in a big deal, plunked down two quarters.

"Hey!" Angie said. "That'll be sixty-two cents, sonny."

The kid scrunched up his freckled nose and with his free hand scratched himself. "That's what my ma give me."

"You tell your ma she owes me twelve cents. Tell her not to send you for anything more until she gives me the twelve cents," Angie told him. The kid made a face and left with the milk tucked under his arm.

"Chiseler," Angie said. "That dame's a chiseler. She knows what milk costs, she figures she sends the kid over, she don't have to pay full price. She's a first-class chiseler, that one."

"Don't let her get away with it," Fex said.

"What're you gonna do?" Angie said. It was her favorite

expression. "What're you gonna do?" she said after her son married a divorced woman ten years older than he was and with four children.

"What're you gonna do?" she asked when fire broke out in her back room and she'd forgotten to renew her insurance and lost a lot of money.

And "What're you gonna do?" she sighed when her husband had a heart attack and the doctor said he might have to have open-heart surgery.

She didn't expect an answer to her eternal question. Fex had figured out that long ago. She kept right on running the store in her son's cut-off army pants, stood guard over the cash register, and kept a sharp eye out for shoplifters.

"O.K., this friend of yours, he's your age, right?"

Fex nodded. "He keeps doing the same dumb thing over and over. He makes a fool of himself and he can't seem to stop."

"I get it!" Angie snapped her fingers. "He's powerless in the grip of his obsession! That's it. When you got an obsession," she told Fex, "it's tough, very tough." Angie was fond of watching soap operas on television. Sometimes she sounded like one of the characters.

"I guess," Fex said. He had no idea what "obsession" meant. But he knew he was powerless.

"An obsession means like he's got to do it. There's something stronger than he is forcing him on, right?"

"That's right," Fex agreed. "That's exactly how it is."

"This friend, he must be a pretty good pal, eh?" Angie asked.

Fex kept his head down and nodded.

"This'll take some thought," Angie said. "Solutions to deep problems don't come easy, you know."

"Tell me," Fex said fervently.

"You don't think you—your friend, that is—could just talk himself outa this thing? Tell himself to shape up. Or maybe he could just grow out of it."

"I doubt it."

"Take my own kid. He had an underwear obsession." Angie tapped herself on the side of her head. "It was all in his mind."

"His underwear obsession was all in his mind?" This was getting more complicated than Fex had bargained for.

"Sure. He thought if he didn't change his underwear it would bring him good luck. He read somewheres that the Chinese or maybe the Irish--I can't remember—had an old superstition that if you didn't change your underwear for a long time—a year maybe—it brought you good luck. So he had an underwear obsession. I thought I'd go nuts. You could smell the kid a mile away."

"What finally happened?"

Angie ate a graham cracker. "Girls," she said. "He got interested in girls. Got so he'd change his underwear six, seven times a day. Couldn't keep up with the wash." She shook her head.

A man came in looking for a screwdriver. "Got some at home, couldn't find a one," he said.

"In the back," Angie directed. "Third drawer on the left. You can't locate what you want, give me a holler."

In a minute he shouted, "Can't find a one!"

"Men." Angie rolled her eyes. "Can't find their elbow unless it's sticking in their eye. I'm coming," she called.

Fex said good-bye and rode his bike slowly, thinking over what she'd said. Halfway home, he felt his rear tire go flat. He got off and pushed.

If I could only shed my skin, he thought, just walk out of it like a snake in the spring, it might be the answer. This was a nice time of year. Everything was starting fresh. Not a bad idea, starting fresh.

The idea of leaving his old self crumpled in a heap by the side of the road, tired and beat up from practically twelve years of strenuous living, and taking on a thin, taut covering like a skindiver's wet suit appealed to him.

There wouldn't be a trace of the old me, he thought, pleased. I would be strong. Nobody could make me do anything I didn't want to do. I would know exactly who I am. I would say the right thing at the right time, do the right thing at the right time. There would be no mistakes. I would never feel foolish again.

I would be my own master. I would be kind. I would think of other people's problems, not just my own. I would be just. I would love my fellowman. I would never hate anyone. I would make God like me.

A tiny voice spoke inside his head.

You might just be a pain in the butt, it told him. If all those things happened, you'd be so perfect it sounds to me like you'd be a real pain in the butt.

Fex paused. "That is a possibility," he said aloud. Still, he couldn't let go. I would be smart. I would be in the top ten percent of my class. Everyone would want me on their team. I might even be rich. And famous.

He stopped pushing his bike. A dazzling picture of himself, rich and famous, overwhelmed him. I might win the lottery. Or the Nobel peace prize. I might discover something that would cure cancer. I might think of a way to eliminate death.

I might even think of an idea that would bring peace to the world.

He stood still. A large Doberman came bounding from behind a picket fence at him, making low noises in its throat. Fex felt the blood drain out of his head and down to his sneakers. He looked at his feet, half expecting to see a pool of blood there. The backs of his hands tingled—a sure sign of danger.

With a trembling hand Fex reached out and touched the dog's warm side.

In a phony English accent he said, "Old boy, how are you? You're looking simply ripping, what?" For some reason the phony accent gave him courage. "Jolly, what, ho ho, pip pip, and all that rot."

The dog looked puzzled, backed off and made more rumbling noises. "You seem to have a touch of indigestion, old thing," Fex said. He kept up the patting. "Where'd you get that kisser?" He kept his voice light, friendly, soothing. "You have a face that only a mother could love, old chap."

The dog put its head to one side, regarded Fex with its flat yellow eyes.

"Buzz off, baby, if you know what's good for you." Fex smiled at his new friend.

The Doberman turned and did as it was told.

Fex was exhilarated by his success. He pushed his bike rapidly the rest of the way and left it in the garage. He had one more thing to do before he went inside. But, no matter how hard he tried, no matter how much he twisted and turned, bent himself out of shape, he found it impossible to stick his elbow in his eye.

Good old Angie.

43

7

"MOM," FEX SAID, TAKING THE BULL BY THE HORNS, "I have to stay after school tomorrow. For a week." Better to get it out of the way before his father came home.

"You can't."

"I have to." Someday he might reach the point where there was no bull whose horns needed taking, Fex thought. Not soon, but someday.

"Why can't I?"

"Dentist's appointment." She sat at the dining room table, taking notes, her office management textbook in front of her. "It's down on the calendar."

"Ma, I've got to."

She sighed and closed her book, marking her place with a piece of scratch paper.

"Why?"

"Because."

"That's no answer."

"I have to work in the principal's office helping Mrs. Timmons for a week. I'm being punished."

"What did you do?"

"Put a drawing on Mr. Palinkas' desk that he didn't like."

She opened her eyes wide. "Why on earth did you do that? I thought you liked him."

"I do, sort of."

"Then why did you want to offend him?"

"I didn't. It turned out that way is all." Why didn't she quit asking him all those questions? His head felt hot, his tongue thick.

"Fex, look at me."

Why did people always want other people to look them straight in the eye? Why couldn't he look over her head? Or close his eyes entirely?

"It was another one of those double-dare things, wasn't it?"

"Yes." It came out as a sigh.

"Ah, Fex." His mother's face wrinkled up. In front of him she seemed to grow older. She looked as if she might cry.

She wasn't a crying type. He knew kids whose mothers burst into tears at the drop of a hat. His mother wasn't like that, thank God. She cried only when she was very mad or when she was very sad. Maybe now she was a bit of both. Don't cry, he told her silently. Please don't.

She sat up very straight, held her head high the way she did when she remembered to do her exercises so she wouldn't get a double chin.

"You'll have to handle it yourself, Fex," she said. "Call the dentist and explain your problem. Maybe they can fit someone else in, on your time. If not, if it's too late, why, you'll just have to pay for the dentist's time, just as if you'd kept your appointment. Out of your own money."

"I bet if I asked Mr. Palinkas if I could start on Monday he'd let me," Fex said. "I don't think he'd mind. What difference does it make to him what day I start? As long as he has me where he wants me."

"What makes you think he wants you in his office every day for a week?" his mother asked. "You handle it any way you can, but I'm not going to lift a finger. It's your baby. Sooner or later, Fex, you've got to come to grips with this insane business." She turned her face away from him.

"Mom," Fex said, "you won't tell Dad, will you?" He wanted to touch her and did not. "He gets so mad."

"Yes," she agreed, "he does. Not without reason. We'll see. You know I don't like to conceal things from him, Fex.

Things that you and the boys do to get yourselves in trouble. The only time I didn't tell him was when you rode your bike up on the parkway on a double-dare." She rested her head on her hand, shading her eyes with it as if to shut out the sight. "I can still hear those brakes, all that terrible squealing of brakes. I said to myself, 'He's dead,' because I thought you were."

"Oh, Mom," Fex said.

His mother walked around inspecting ash trays to see if they were clean. Then she plumped up the pillows on the couch. Fex stayed where he was because he knew she wasn't through with him. There was no sense in leaving the room. She was building up to something, and he might as well see it through.

She gave a pillow a savage punch.

"I thought you were over this," she said. "I thought all this was behind you. Us." She stopped what she was doing and became very still. They watched each other in the silence.

"I'm not sure I can cope with any more of your double-dare foolishness," Fex's mother said slowly. "I don't think I can. If I could help, I would. If you could tell me what's bothering you, Fex, maybe I could be of some help."

"There's nothing bothering me, Ma," he said, hunching his shoulders. He felt as if he were back in Mr. Palinkas' office. How come everyone wants to know if there's something bothering me? he asked himself irritably. I'm O.K.

"All right," she said after a minute. "You're on your own. All I know is you have to be at the dentist's office tomorrow afternoon. If you also have to be in the principal's office, I guess you'll have to straighten out your conflict of interests by yourself. I've got some studying to do," she said and left him alone, sitting on the end of his spine, feeling lower than a snake.

I wonder if she's going to tell Dad? Fex thought. Probably she will. Oh, man. I can hear the lecture now. It ought to be good for at least an hour, maybe more. He sighed a deep, scratchy sigh. "You're on your own," she'd said. O.K. So he was. So what?

NEXT MORNING FEX WOKE EARLY, EVEN BEFORE THE birds. And in Connecticut, in late May, that's early. The sun fought its way over the horizon; thick mist lay everywhere. When he went out, he'd better go barefoot. No sense in soaking his sneakers.

Fex put his hands behind his head and looked at the wallpaper. Overhead, Jerry slept quietly.

Fex had never been able to understand why he always woke so early on the days when he expected trouble. This day he'd have to face Mr. Palinkas, who would look at him over his glasses, rummage through his hair, and give him a hard time. Yet, when the dawn broke on an unbearably exciting day, a day on which something great was going to happen, he overslept. It didn't make sense. Take the time their father was taking the three boys on a fishing trip. He'd overslept. Imagine that. The first time they'd ever gone off without their mother and he'd overslept so that he ate his breakfast so fast he'd felt sick throughout most of the journey. He hadn't gotten sick; he'd just felt sick. Hard to say which was worse.

He studied the bare spots where long strips of wallpaper were missing. Jerry and he had peeled the strips off when they hadn't had anything else to do. Sometimes it was hard work, peeling off wallpaper. The one who managed to pull off the longest unbroken strip won. There'd been discussions of new wallpaper down the years, always rejected as being too expensive.

"We'll wait until they go to college," Mr. O'Toole had decided. "By then they'll be too old for the clowns anyway."

Little did he know. They were too old for the clowns right now.

Fex lay looking at the balloon-like faces with great fat pink cheeks. Maybe they all had the mumps. He wondered if he'd ever liked that wallpaper, even when he was little. He thought probably not. Jerry said that wallpaper gave him the creeps. "All those faces watching me," he'd complained to Fex. "Night and day they're up there, giving me the eyeball. I'd like to push 'em through to the other side of the wall." But he never had.

The sun finally popped out from behind the early morning clouds. Fex threw on some jeans and a T-shirt and slipped out into the day, careful not to disturb anyone. He loved being out in the morning alone. No people, no cars, no nothing. He always hoped he might see a deer. Possible but not probable in this part of the world.

It was going to be a perfect day. The air was sparkling, filled with the promise of joy. He would make it a joyous day. No matter what. It was as if he were alone in the world.

Except for Charlie. Early as it was, Charlie Soderstrom was there, squatting on his haunches by the edge of the river, muttering to himself. Fex slithered down the side of the hill, leaving snail tracks on the grass as he made his way through the heavy dew.

"Hi," said Charlie. "I saw a fish."

"Go get some clothes on before you freeze to death," Fex said. Charlie's bare stomach poked out over the elastic of his underpants. They and a sock were all he had on.

"O.K.," he said and churned across the yard to his house. Fex liked to watch him run. He seemed to move up and down more than forward, but he got where he was going, which was what counted.

Presently Charlie returned, carrying a bunch of stuff. "Want some help?" Fex asked.

"No!" Charlie bellowed. He thrashed around inside his sweater for a while and finally figured out where he should put his head and his arms. "See, I told you I could do it myself!" he crowed triumphantly.

"Not bad. Not half bad. Now why don't you see if your mother's got any good grub to eat?" Fex suggested.

"O.K.," Charlie said. Fex lay back on the grass to wait for him.

Am I powerless in the grip of an obsession, the way Angie said? he asked himself. And answered, truthfully, I don't know. If only I lived in the olden days, he thought, as he often had. Not so much hassle. No obsessions, no pollution. Life was easier then. Reading by candlelight, no staying after school, no talk of "putting out" and "getting any." Horses instead of cars. I bet those guys never heard of a double-dare. And if they did, they'd flatten the guys who double-dared 'em. Boy, those were the days.

You take Johnny Tremain. Or Uncas. Or Rolf in the Woods. Fex sat up and thought about spearing fish for breakfast, about catching and skinning muskrats to sell the skins. That was the way to live. Those guys had it made.

He watched as Charlie struggled toward him, carrying a large load of things he'd taken from his mother's kitchen. Maybe I should help him, Fex thought. No. On second thought, let him do it on his own. It's the only way he'll learn.

9

"MRS. TIMMONS, I HAVE A DENTIST'S APPOINTMENT today. My mother made it a long time ago," Fex said. "Can I start Monday instead?"

"Why"—Mrs. Timmons looked up from her type-writer—"I don't know why not. He isn't in yet, but the minute he gets here, I'll ask him. Can you stop back in about an hour?"

"Sure. Thanks."

"I'm sorry about the whole thing, Fex." Mrs. Timmons grabbed for her pencil, which seemed to grow behind her ear. She worried it around in her hair like a dog with a bone. "I was the one who said I'd seen you coming from the office yesterday. That's how Mr. Palinkas knew it was you who'd put the drawing there. I suppose I shouldn't have said I'd seen you."

"If you saw me, you saw me," Fex said. "It doesn't matter."

"Yes, it does," she said. "It matters to me. I hate to see you in trouble, Fex. Why did you do such a senseless thing?"

"I don't know," Fex said.

"Next time you're tempted to do something foolish, think twice." She pushed her chair away from her desk and stood up. "Mr. Palinkas is a good man, a good principal. He cares about all you kids. He doesn't need to be paid back in insults and childish pranks."

The door opened. Mr. Palinkas came in. He raised his eyebrows and poked his stick in Fex's direction. "I said after school, not before." He took off his gray hat, which always looked as if he'd sat on it, and hung it on a hook. "Good morning, Mrs. Timmons," he said.

Mrs. Timmons laid her hand on Fex's shoulder. "He has a dentist's appointment today that his mother made some time ago, and he wondered if he could start work on Monday."

"You tell 'em why you have to stay after school?" Mr. Palinka punctuated his words with little jabs of his stick.

"Yes," Fex said, forgetting the "sir."

"How'd they feel about it?"

"My mother was upset. She said it was dumb."

"How about your father?"

"I didn't tell my father. Just my mother. My father gets really sore when he hears I did something like that. So I didn't tell him," Fex said, his voice belligerent. At least I'm not lying, he wanted to say. At least I'm telling you the truth. I could've lied. Give me credit for that.

Mr. Palinkas nodded. "You've done this kind of thing before, then?" he asked.

"Well, not exactly. But a couple of times when kids dared me, I've done some dumb things, and that really makes him mad."

He hadn't meant to say that about someone daring him. But it was out. He couldn't call it back.

"Did someone dare you to put that picture on my desk?" Mr. Palinkas seemed genuinely interested.

"Yes, sir." If he asks me who, I won't tell him, Fex decided.

"I see." Mr. Palinkas sat down heavily in his big swivel chair. "It's not a new concept, you know. Daring people to do things you don't dare to do yourself."

"I suppose not." Fex had never thought of it quite that way. But that was true. Barney dared him to do things he wouldn't dare to do himself. That put things in a different light. As Audrey would say, he was a fall guy. A first-class jerk of a fall guy.

"It's a coward's trick. It always amazes me to realize how many cowards there are around. The world's full of them." Mr. Palinkas took a cigarette lighter out of his pocket and snapped it on and off several times.

"Gave it up," he said. "I'm trying to stick to it. But it isn't easy. Not at all. Don't know if I can do it. My wife gives me a hard time. She hates the smell of cigarette smoke. Says I should have enough strength of character to quit for good." Again he snapped his lighter. "I've given up smoking three times," he told them, shaking his head. A small silence fell on the room.

"It's all right, is it then, Mr. Palinkas, if Fex starts Monday?" Mrs. Timmons said in a bright voice.

"Yes, it's all right. Monday's fine." Mr. Palinkas pulled at his nose, then looked down at his jacket and brushed at it as if he'd spilled something on himself.

There didn't seem to be anything more to say.

Mrs. Timmons nodded to Fex. "See you then," she said.

"Thank you," Fex said. "Thanks a lot." He backed out and stumbled over the doorsill.

Mr. Palinkas looked up.

"Better watch your step," he said.

"Yes, sir." Fex turned and ran.

10

LONG AGO, WHEN HE'D BEEN SMALL ENOUGH TO FIT neatly under his mother's arm as she read to him before bedtime (and sometimes she read to him in the middle of the day, for no reason at all), she'd read him a tale about a baby who had been born under a cabbage leaf. Left there by the fairies, the baby had been picked up, nourished, and cared for by an old couple with no children of their own. When this cabbage leaf baby became a man, he was good and noble and did all sorts of good and noble things.

At times, Fex liked to think that he too had been born under a cabbage leaf. It seemed to him a quaint and original way to come into the world. Never mind the tiny bracelet made of blue beads, reading "O'Toole," which his mother assured him had once fitted around his wrist as he lay in the hospital nursery—placed there by diligent nurses so he wouldn't get mixed up and go home with the wrong family.

Never mind the birth certificate stating that one Francis Xavier O'Toole, sex male, had been born on June 27 at 1:50 P.M. That struck him as odd. He'd always understood that babies arrived in the middle of the night. But there it was: 1:50 P.M. The sun had been shining brightly, his mother said, on the day he was born. People were going to the movies at 1:50 P.M. Or coming back from lunch. Or standing up in English class trying to remember the poem they were supposed to have memorized the night before.

There was a picture on his father's dresser of Pete, aged three and a bit, and an ancient girl cousin, at least ten years old, holding him, Fex, a wizened, wrinkled baby, up for the camera's inspection—holding him as if he were a bomb that might go off at any minute. Passing him back and forth between them as if he were a football.

No cabbage leaf baby ever got that kind of treatment.

He didn't look like anyone. Not his mother, who was fair with blue eyes. People were always saying Jerry looked like her. When he heard that, Fex pushed down the terrible pangs of jealousy he felt. He longed for someone to say that he, Fex, looked like his mother. Was, in fact, the image of her. No one ever did.

And he certainly didn't resemble his father, who looked rather like pictures Fex had seen of Abraham Lincoln. Fex thought his father was cool looking. He wished he looked like him. And he didn't even look like his brothers. Not Jerry the violinist with the face of innocence and sweetness that made him the old ladies' darling. And not Pete, who was tall for his age, good-looking and filled with aggressive self-confidence. Pete had curly brown hair and had never wondered for a moment where he was going, who he was. Things would most likely turn out the way he'd planned them for the simple reason that Pete wouldn't have it any other way. People like Pete had a head start on life, Fex figured. Pete was off and running before he, Fex, had even warmed up.

They had never been friends, he and Pete. Sometimes Fex thought they weren't really brothers at all. Weren't even related to each other. That's when he pulled the cabbage leaf theory out and examined it. Suppose those little blue beads that spelled out his name were lying. Suppose in the night someone had sneaked into the hospital nursery and switched the bracelets and he was really someone else. Stranger things have happened. All you had to do was read the newspapers and you'd know that.

If I could pick my family, Fex thought, I'd keep my mother and father, and I'd trade in Pete. Maybe for

Audrey. And keep Jerry, of course. Even with his practicing, I'd hang on to Jerry.

These were the things he sometimes thought about. Along with lots of other things. But when he was about to dip into sleep, thoughts swirled through his head that he couldn't always remember the next day. It infuriated him, especially when he knew they'd been exciting or original ideas or mind pictures which, if he could only bring them back into focus, might be worth keeping. Once, for instance, he'd slipped over the edge of sleep just as he saw himself, perfectly clearly, dressed in a red uniform with brass buttons and a steel helmet that glinted in the sun. People were lined up on either side as he rode his magnificent black stallion into town. Girls threw rose petals in his path, and shouts of "O'Toole! O'Toole!" rang in his ears. That had definitely been worth pursuing.

Suddenly, unbidden, lines from one of his father's favorite poems, one he sometimes recited, came to Fex's mind.

"I am the master of my fate," the poem went, "I am the captain of my soul." He thought about that. The captain of my soul. That would be nice—to be the captain of your own soul. He wondered how a person managed that. For one thing, if he wanted to achieve it, he'd have to give up on the double-dare stuff.

When had it started? Why? He thought back to the first

time. He'd been five. They'd been in the five-and-ten shopping for stuff the day before Easter. The store was crowded with people buying candy and baskets and straw hats. Out of the blue, Pete had dared him to walk down the center aisle of the store on his hands. He'd just learned how to walk on his hands and was very proud of himself. He'd done pretty well, falling down only when he got to the notions counter. He remembered the look on his mother's face as she turned to see what all the noise, the applause, the commotion was about. Even the manager of the store had joined in on the applause. It was a wonderful moment.

"Little showoff," Pete had muttered. That had been the beginning. Fex couldn't let go. He liked to make people laugh. He felt important. From then on, Fex was hooked. Kids found out and double-dared him to do crazy things, dangerous things. Once he'd jumped off the jungle gym at school when a kid dared him, and he'd broken his collarbone. Another time when he was about eight, a gang of kids had been down by the river. It was March, and the ice that had formed during the cold winter was thin. They had thought they could see fish swimming underneath. A kid had said, "Double-dare you, Fex, to walk on that ice," and, not even thinking, he'd started across to the other side. The ice was green and gray, and it creaked under his feet. He'd almost made it. Then the ice had given way with a kind of creaking sigh, throwing him into water so cold he couldn't even cry out. The kids standing there on the shore, watching him, were scared. A couple of them ran away. But luck was with him. A man in a truck heard the others hollering for help, and he stopped and ran down to the riverbank carrying a large, stout rope from his truck. Fex caught the rope on the first try, and the man hauled him to safety.

That should've cured him. But no. He let his father think he'd fallen in by accident. From his mother's face, he was sure she knew the truth. She tried to talk to him, asked him why he let himself be used by other kids.

"Please, Fex," she begged, sitting on the edge of his bunk. "Promise me you won't do any of that daredevil stuff. Promise me. I worry about you." But, no matter how hard she begged, he never really promised her because he knew he'd break that promise. Sooner or later he'd break it.

His father got very angry with him. He lectured Fex a long time about growing up, taking responsibility (that word again) for his own actions. When the police had brought Fex home after the bike riding incident on the parkway, his father had been home, raking leaves. The policeman explained what had happened. His father was very polite, said thank you to the policeman. "Come inside," he'd said then to Fex, his face tight, grim. "I want to talk to you."

He'd paced back and forth in the living room. "You know you might have been killed, don't you?" he'd said. His voice rose, gained strength and ferocity. "It was another of those dares, wasn't it, that made you do that damn fool thing?" Fex had never seen him so angry. He'd nodded, too scared to speak.

His father lectured him for what seemed like hours. His mother cried a lot. But when her tears dried, she was just as angry as his father. Later she calmed down. "You promised me you wouldn't do those things any more," she'd said.

"I never promised, Mom," he'd said. "I don't know what makes me do those crazy dumb things. I try not to. But every time I do." Then she kissed him, and he felt her cheek wet against his. He felt terrible, but that night he'd had a vivid dream. All his dreams were vivid, but this one took the cake. He was swinging on a trapeze without a net because someone had double-dared him. He looked down and heard the roar of the crowd, saw their faces turned up to watch him. When he started a spectacular triple somersault, they rose to their feet and screamed with excitement. He looked down and saw there was no net. Then he woke up. He never found out if he made it, but boy, it had been exciting!

The next morning his father had said, "I will say only one more thing on the subject and then we'll let it rest." Fex hoped that this was so but knew it wasn't. Through tight lips, his father said, "Only fools accept dares to do things that might result in injury or death. Remember that the next time someone double-dares you, Fex. Remember that."

And he'd tried. He really had tried.

11

SATURDAY OPENED LIKE A HUGE SUNFLOWER, ALL yellow and green. It was a day to spend carefully, like hard-earned money. Which was what none of them had.

Audrey and Fex were cold stone broke. They stood on the corner, discussing plans.

Then, in her cool way, Audrey said, "Let's go see Angie."

Angie was there, as usual. Behind the cash register, guarding the money, keeping a wary eye out for shoplifters.

"How's it going?" Fex said to her. "How ya doing?"

She considered this. "You know what the definition of a bore is, right? It's somebody who, when you ask 'em how they're doing, they tell you. So I'm gonna tell you. My feet hurt, the mortgage is due, my mother-in-law is coming to live with us, and the cat just had kittens. Outside of that, everything's hunky-dory." She threw back her head and laughed. Her glasses flew off. "Uh-oh," she said, bending down to pick them up. Miraculously, they hadn't broken.

"What're you gonna do?" Angie said. She dusted off her glasses and put them back on.

Once, long ago, Angie had left Fex in charge of the store while she ran across the street to the bakery. She liked the doughnuts they made there better than the ones she sold, she said. Fex had crossed his arms on his chest and stood his vigil, ready to fight anyone who tried to rob the joint. No one had, no one had even come in to buy anything, but how did he know that? He'd felt like the Incredible Hulk standing there, muscles bulging, prepared for the worst.

In payment Angie had given him a free Coke and a bag of Fritos. Nothing he'd eaten before or since had ever tasted sweeter.

"How's your husband?" Fex asked Angie. He'd forgotten to ask the other day when they'd had their obsession talk.

"Legs aren't what they used to be," Angie said. "He runs out of steam early on. Hits the sack about nine, ten o'clock. Doesn't even go bowling any more. And him a young man still, sixty-four in July." She shook her head. "But he's alive. You count your blessings, right?"

They nodded in agreement. The door opened and Mr. Soderstrom came in, trailed by Charlie.

"Fex." Mr. Soderstrom bowed in his direction, his vast beard fanning out over his shirtfront. "Just the fellow I was looking for. Could you manage to look after this young man"—his huge hand rested lightly on Charlie's head, the thick fingers hanging down on Charlie's forehead like some weird sort of hat—"next Saturday? Company wedding. Fancy dress affair. Mrs. S. says we must go."

"Sure, be glad to," Fex said.

"Hi, Fex." Charlie played it smooth, acting as if he came to the general store every day of his life.

"Hi, Charlie." Fex played it just as cool.

Mr. Soderstrom was almost entirely bald except for his luxuriant beard, which, Fex had noticed, collected all sorts of things: tobacco, cookie crumbs, bits and pieces of potato chips, of which he was fond. If some small creature ever got caught inside Mr. Soderstrom's beard, Fex thought, it could probably survive for a long time, eating the stuff that collected there. He could almost see the small face peering out, nose twitching, as it caught the thousands of crumbs that daily filtered through. He imagined Mr. Soderstrom kissing Mrs. S.—as he called his wife—and having the creature pop out, sending her screaming, the daylights scared out of her. She'd never kiss him again without checking his beard first.

"Peat moss," Mr. Soderstrom muttered. "You have peat moss?"

"Twenty-five-pound bags," Angie said. "In the back. Four-fifty per."

Mr. Soderstrom reared back as if she'd struck him. "Four-fifty!" he roared.

Angie shrugged. "Everything's gone up," she said.

Sighing loudly, talking to himself, Mr. Soderstrom lugged a bag of peat moss to the cash register.

Angie rang it up. "Add the gum to your bill?" she asked.

"Gum? Gum? I didn't buy any gum!"

Angie pointed to Charlie, who had filched a pack of Wrigley's spearmint and was passing out sticks like Santa Claus handing out presents.

"The kid's lightfingered," Mr. Soderstrom grumbled. "Takes after my wife's brother." Then he felt the need to repeat himself. "My wife's brother!" he roared, in case anyone had missed it.

After the noise had died down, Angie pointed to Charlie and said, "I hardly recognized him, he got so big."

"They grow up too fast," Mr. Soderstrom said gloomily. He'd confided to Fex that he had two teenaged children from his first marriage. "Like 'em better when they're young," he'd said. "If I could, I'd freeze this fellow right where he is now. Four's a wonderful age. He thinks I'm great, I think he's great. They grow up, they start finding fault with the old man."

He shouldered the bag of peat moss. "Oh, they grow up too fast," he repeated, shaking his head ruefully.

"Want some help?" Fex asked.

"Oh, I'm not over the hill yet, my boy!" he cried. "Not by a long shot. Come on, Charlie. Get a move on. See you Saturday, Fex. Mrs. S. will let you know what time."

"So long," Charlie said, deftly slipping another pack of Wrigley's spearmint into his pocket.

Angie lifted her shoulders.

"What're you gonna do?" she said.

12

DINNER THAT NIGHT WAS SWEET-AND-SOUR PORK. FEX gorged himself. Jerry leaned on his elbow when his father wasn't looking, pushing bits of pineapple around his plate, as if they were racing cars and the plate the track.

"May I please be excused?" Pete said. When his manners were good, it was a sign of big things. Pete was going to a dance at the high school.

"Who's your date?" Mrs. O'Toole asked.

"Date?" Pete mouthed the word as if it were distasteful to him. "*Date?* You must be kidding, Mom. Nobody has dates for a dance."

"In my day," said Mr. O'Toole, "it was considered standard practice to ask a young lady to a dance. Otherwise you'd have to dance by yourself, and that might cause talk. Whom do you dance with if you don't bring a date?"

"We mess around, see what we can dig up when we get there," Pete said. "The girls come in a crowd, we come in a crowd. Some kids disco. The rest sort of mill around, you know?"

"No," said Mr. O'Toole. "I'm not sure I do."

"I thought you liked that nice Butler girl," Mrs. O'Toole said. "She seemed sweet the one time I met her. Why not ask her?"

Pete rolled his eyes and said nothing.

"Be home by eleven," Mr. O'Toole said.

"Dad!" Pete smacked his forehead with enough force to knock himself to the floor. "Dad, the dance isn't over until eleven. Make it twelve? Please?" He shot a pleading glance at his mother, which she ignored.

"I'll compromise. Eleven-thirty. That'll give you ample time. Especially as you don't have to see a date to her front door."

"You boobed that one," Fex said under his breath.

Later, he leaned on the bathroom door, watching Pete lavish his father's after-shave on his face, then do the same with hair tonic, coating each strand of hair with great care.

"How come you didn't ask a girl to the dance?" Fex asked.

"You think I'm taking some girl out and have us sit in the

back seat while the old man drives us to the door?" Pete squeezed toothpaste on his brush. He was going all-out tonight. "I know guys who do that. Once. Only once. They sweat buckets. The girl's making conversation with the old man, and the guy sits there like some super nerd. No dates for me until I get my license. Then I get behind the wheel and spin over to the chick's house and load her inside and take off. Once you got wheels, your sex life begins," he finished, leering.

Fex figured if he kept his mouth shut, he might learn something. "Oh, yeah," he said noncommittally.

"You know about sex, baby brother? The birds and the bees?" Pete admired his muscles in the mirror. "You ever make out with a girl?" he said.

"I'm not even twelve yet!" Fex protested. "Whadya want?"

"By the time I was your age"—Pete's hands were suspended over his coiffure—"I was an old hand at making out. Some guys got it, some don't."

"Who'd you make out with?" Fex said.

"A gentleman never tells."

"Do girls like to make out? Did she like it, the girl you made out with?"

Pete rolled back his lips and studied his gums in the mirror. "Girls, sonny, girls," he said at last. "You better believe they did. All of 'em," he said, leering again. "But you need practice. You don't just all of a sudden lunge at a chick and say, 'This is it, babe.' She might deck you. You gotta be subtle."

Fex held his breath, afraid the sound of his breathing might stop the flow of Pete's advice.

Who do I practice on? he asked himself. Just who?

"Practice makes perfect," Pete continued. "You put the moves on a girl, you better know where it's at. For instance." He stared hard at Fex. "You know how to French kiss?"

"French kiss? I don't even know how to American kiss," Fex answered.

"O.K. for you, wise guy. Think you're funny, think it's a big joke," Pete said angrily. Fex hadn't meant to be funny.

"I speak from experience, remember. The best teacher, right?" Pete put on his blue sweater, his face flushed. "You gotta know the ropes before you can swing, kid. Take it from one who knows. You gotta know the ropes before you can swing."

He whipped off his blue sweater and changed to his tan one. It's lucky he only has two sweaters, Fex thought, watching, or he'd never make the dance at all.

"But where do I start? I mean, how do I start?"

Pete frowned. "Maybe she'll do the starting. Maybe she'll put the moves on you. If she's hot for your bod, that's probably what'll happen. Women's lib, you know." Looking very wise, Pete changed back into the blue sweater.

"It's all in the timing," he said, pushing up his sleeves. "If her folks hang around, the little brother wants you to assemble his model airplane, you've had it. But if they go off to play bridge, watch the tube, then you've got it made."

"I do?"

"Sure." Satisfied at last with his appearance, Pete made for the door. He left a strong odor of hair tonic, toothpaste, and after-shave in his wake.

"That's when you blow in her ear. Put your hand on her leg and blow in her ear. Then see what happens. Well, I'm off. Don't wait up." And he was gone.

Fex sat where he was, pulling himself together. He heard the front door slam, heard Pete whistling as he went down the walk. Then, moving as quietly as a burglar out for the flat silver, Fex went downstairs. His mother and father and Jerry were still in the kitchen. He could hear them talking and laughing. He went to the dictionary to look up French kiss. It said, "See soul kiss." He looked up soul kiss. If it said, "See French kiss," he'd have to throw in the towel. But luck was with him. The dictionary defined soul kiss as "An open-mouth kiss in which the tongue of one partner is manipulated in the mouth of the other." Fortunately, "manipulate" was spelled exactly the way it sounded. It meant, "To handle, manage, or use with skill," the dictionary said. As he understood it, that meant you put your tongue in the girl's mouth and then used it with skill. Sort of like a Water Pik, Fex told himself, making a face. Gross. Really gross. Forget it. I'm not getting into any of that stuff.

"Fex! Telephone!" his father called.

"Thanks, Dad. Hello," Fex said into the phone.

"Hi. Want to come over and watch TV? I'm baby-sitting. There's going to be a cool program on about the spirit world. Mom says it's O.K. if you come over for a while."

It was Audrey. Asking him to come over and watch TV. Her parents were obviously going out.

"Sure," Fex said after a pause. "I guess so." He hung up and studied the toe of his sneakers. The left one had a rip in the fabric. If he taped the rip, he could wear the sneaker a lot longer. On the other hand, if the rip got bigger he'd have to buy a new pair. He decided to try the tape. Painstakingly he put three strips of tape over the hole.

Jerry came in. "I can't decide whether I want to watch TV or practice," Jerry said.

"Why not do both?" Fex asked. Jerry looked puzzled. That's what I'm doing, Fex thought. "Both!" Fex said aloud. "I'm going to Audrey's to watch TV, so the joint's yours."

"How can I do both at the same time?" Jerry said. "You're nuts."

Fex didn't answer. He ran down to tell his mother and

father where he was going. As he rushed out into the gentle night air, he heard Jerry starting to make his coyote-caught-in-a-trap noises. Halfway to Audrey's he slowed down. He didn't want to look too eager.

13

EMMA ANSWERED THE DOOR. SHE WAS NAKED, AS usual.

"Hi," she said.

Emma was Audrey's sister. Half sister. Audrey's parents had been divorced when she was little. Four years ago her mother had remarried. Emma was three.

"Where's Audrey?" Fex said. He was used to Emma by now.

"Taking a bath," Em said. She wasn't completely naked. On her feet she wore a pair of ancient black rubbers. They were enormous. She maneuvered the rubbers as if they were skis and she were preparing for a downhill run. She pointed them in the direction she wanted to go, then followed them.

Emma walked nonchalantly past Fex on her way outside. The old lady who lived next door was probably stationed at her window in her nocturnal vigil. Fex knew she'd threatened to call the authorities several times if Emma continued to walk around unclothed.

Fex watched as Em made her way majestically across the lawn. If the mosquitoes discovered her, she'd be a goner.

"Go in if you want," she called over her bare shoulder. Em had a mind of her own.

"Oh, Lord." It was Audrey's mother in her robe, with curlers in her hair. "Will you get her please, Fex?"

"Shall I just grab her or what?"

"Here." She handed him a wilted half sandwich. "It's mayonnaise and ketchup, her favorite. Sometimes it works, sometimes not. Try, would you?"

Feeling a fool one more time, Fex caught up with Emma. It wasn't hard. She wasn't making very good time. He held the sandwich just out of reach.

"Mayo and ketchup, Em," he said, suppressing a desire to add, "Yum-yum." There were certain lengths to which he would not go.

Emma came to a halt. The rubbers quivered in the still evening air. She put out her hand. Fex moved the bait out of her reach.

"Please." She smiled at him.

"Your mother wants you inside," he said. Emma sighed. She knew when she was licked. She turned toward home, handling the rubbers as if she were the ship's captain and about to bring the *Queen Elizabeth* into port. One rubber fell off. Em sat down on the grass to put it back on. She managed. It was a rare sight, seeing her get to her feet. Slowly, holding out the sandwich like a bone before a reluctant dog, Fex, with Emma bringing up the rear, inched his way toward the house.

With his foot on the top step, Fex glanced toward the old lady's house. The curtains moved as if caught in a strong wind. Fex smiled. Lucky he got Em back in so fast. Who knows? The old lady might've called the fire department. She had, more than once.

Fex lifted a hand and waved in her direction. The curtains stopped swaying and fell into place. Like most spies, the old lady didn't like to be caught in the act.

"Hello, Fex." Audrey's stepfather greeted him. "You here to help tend the Mighty Mite?" That's what he called Emma. He was a nice man. Audrey called him Tom, which was his name. Her real father had also remarried and had three kids. Audrey had a passel of half brothers and sisters. They all got on together. She liked her stepmother, too. Fex was envious. He would have liked to have had a half brother or sister or two. His family was too ordinary, he thought. It would be pleasant to have a mixed-up family.

"We're going across the street to the Kellmans' to play bridge," Audrey's mother said. "Read Em a *Curious George* story before she goes to bed, will you? That always calms her down."

"She knows *Curious George* by heart," Audrey said. "Hi, Fex. I can hardly wait to see this program. It's about the spirit world and how dead people come back and give messages to their loved ones."

Fex tried to conceal the shudder that ran over him. He wasn't keen on knowing more about the spirit world. But he'd just as soon no one, especially Audrey, found out.

"Don't forget to lock up when Fex leaves, Aud," her mother said. "We won't be late. We have our key."

Audrey took Em up to bed. Downstairs, Fex paced. It was now or never. Practice makes perfect, doesn't it?

"She wants you to make her a boat out of newspaper," Audrey said when she came down. "Like the one *Curious George* makes." O.K. He'd make the kid a paper boat.

He made her three. Em clamored for more. He told her no, three was it.

His mouth was filled with saliva. No matter how often he swallowed, it wouldn't go away. He ran his finger around the collar of his T-shirt. It felt tight, as if his neck had expanded.

"This is going to be cool," Audrey said, adjusting the

color. She plumped down beside him on the couch.

"Want some potato chips?" she asked, holding out the bag. He shook his head. He couldn't eat anything. His tongue felt swollen in his mouth, as if it had been bitten by some strange off-course bee. With his mouth filled with saliva and his tongue taking up the rest of the space, he better forget the French kiss. Start someplace else.

"Blow in her ear," Pete had said. Fex looked at Audrey. She needed a haircut. Ordinarily her ears were in plain sight. Now they were shrouded in hair. How could he see where to blow?

I'm not up to this, he thought sorrowfully. I've bitten off more than I can chew. A picture sprang into his mind, a picture of him biting off a piece of Audrey's ear and trying to chew it. Her ear was tough. He started to laugh, then he felt sick.

Eerie music came from the TV set. Someone screamed. He hoped it hadn't been him. Audrey chomped on potato chips, spraying crumbs.

"Neat," she murmured, scrooching down as the announcer's juicy voice told them they were about to be introduced to something marvelously weird.

You ain't seen nothing, bud, Fex thought. Tentatively he moved his arm so it rested on the back of the couch. He let his fingers walk unsteadily toward their goal.

He touched Audrey's neck. Gently he let them stay

where they'd landed. She took an absentminded swipe at the spot, eyes riveted on the TV. Fex moved closer. He let his other hand rest lightly on her denimed knee, as if by accident. Things were going better than he'd expected. Credits flashed on the screen: credits to the director, the actors, the producer. A long list. Audrey jumped up and ran to the kitchen. Fex felt as if God had given him a reprieve, as if he'd been on death row and the governor had just commuted his sentence. She came back with a bag of Cheez-O's and two Cokes.

You mean I have to start all over again? Fex asked himself. Man, there's more to this stuff than they let on. Much more. He felt like a paratrooper about to make his first jump.

Again he let his hand creep up on her. His arm went around her neck. She looked at him from the corner of her eye, which glowed red in the light from the TV set.

"What's up?" she inquired.

He grabbed her around her neck. Her little bones lay so close under her skin it seemed possible they might pierce through and scratch his hand. Her face was turned to him, incredulous. He opened his mouth and aimed for hers. He missed. His mouth skidded off her slick cheek like a car off an icy road.

His face plunged into the soft, rough fabric of the couch. He could hardly breathe. He felt as if he were being smothered. Maybe Audrey had decided to kill him.

"You're cuckoo," he heard her say. Her voice sounded faraway. More screams came from the spirit world, followed by moans.

"That's all you are is cuckoo."

He lay still, wondering what to do now.

He wished for nothing but escape. He longed to run for cover, to dig a hole and hide. For a long, long time.

Silence engulfed him. She must've turned off the TV. Slowly he raised his head. He knew he was being watched.

Emma stood in the doorway in her nightgown. For a minute Fex didn't recognize her. He wasn't used to seeing her in clothes.

Eyes glowing like two beacons in the darkness, Emma said, "Wotcha doing?" In her long white gown she looked like a plump little wraith.

Audrey was gone. Probably in the kitchen calling her parents to tell them to come home quick to rescue her from a sex maniac. Fex pulled himself together.

Emma put her head to one side, studying him. "Wotcha doing?" she said again. Fex shook his head.

"Nothing," he said in a weak voice. "I have to go. Go back to bed, Em. Tell Audrey I have to go home."

He fought his way out into the night. It was soft and cool and filled with stars. He wished it were raining.

At home he lay awake for hours, staring up at Jerry's

backside. He'd never be able to face her again. He wondered if she'd tell anyone and hoped she wouldn't. Then, as he began the long, steep slide into sleep, he thought, I don't want to grow up. I'm not ready. I don't think I can handle it.

14

DURING THE NIGHT THE FOG ROLLED IN. OUTSIDE, a bird shrieked, confused, perhaps, by the swirling grayness. Fex sat up in bed the next morning and listened to the buzzing sound Jerry made when he snored. Like a mosquito looking for a square meal.

Fex got up and peered out the window. Maybe he'd died during the night and the spirits waited out there, ready to claim him.

No such luck. He got dressed, left a note on the kitchen table to say where he'd gone, and rode his bike to church. Once there, he locked his bike, went inside, and sat in the back pew. Sometimes he derived a sense of peace and contentment from church. Not today. When the collection plate was passed, he stared stonily down at his hands. He had no money to give. Afterward he rode around the quiet streets and eventually wound up at the general store. Thick stacks of Sunday papers lay on the sidewalk where the driver had dumped them. The store was locked. On the spur of the moment Fex decided to ride over to Angie's. She'd told him to drop in when he was in the neighborhood. He only had to make a slight detour to get to her neighborhood.

Angie's house was thin and dark, like Angie herself. She and her husband owned it, had paid off the mortgage last year, she'd told Fex. They lived on the top floor and rented out the ground floor to a family with a bunch of kids. The yard was dotted with tricycles and skateboards and mounds of plastic soldiers, much like Charlie's, lying in a trench someone had carved out of the packed-down dirt around the porch. Again Fex locked his bike. He took the outside stairs two at a time.

In answer to his knock a voice called, "Who's there?"

"It's me, Fex O'Toole," he said.

The door opened a crack. "Come on in," Angie said. He followed her into the kitchen. She had on a long pink bathrobe and fuzzy purple slippers that looked like miniature dust mops.

"I'm making bacon," she said. "Sit yourself down and make yourself homely.

"It's a good thing you stopped by," she told him as he sat down at the kitchen table. "I'm making pancakes, and I always make too much batter and have to toss it out. My husband watches what he eats."

Fex didn't know how to start, how to say what he wanted to say.

"Get the butter out of the refrigerator, O.K.?" she said. "And pour out some syrup. There's a pitcher right there. My husband's still in the sack. He needs a lot of rest since his attack." She piled two plates high with pancakes and decorated the edges of the plates with strips of bacon.

"Looks good enough to eat, eh?" she said, setting the plates down. In the center of the table, which was covered with a red-and-white-checked cloth, she put a container of milk, as if it were a bowl of flowers.

"O.K., we're set," and they ate in a companionable silence. When he'd eaten all he could manage, Fex said, "How come you're not at the store by now?"

Angie shrugged. "I hired a guy to come in Sundays, to take charge until I get there. I'm wearing myself to a frazzle. My husband gives me a hard time, says we should sell out, retire to Florida. Can you see me in Florida? Me in my bikini?" She hooted with laughter.

"Who wants to retire to Florida? Not me. In Florida you got yourself a bunch of senior citizens playing shuffleboard and talking about all those ailments you see on TV.

Irregularity, dentures, indigestion. How to make yourself old before your time.

"And anyway, who thought up that senior citizen bit? What does that make you?" She pointed at Fex. "Are you a junior citizen? Or maybe a kid citizen. I think they got their nerve. I'm no senior citizen. What's more, I don't ever plan on being one. Not if I live to be a hundred. It's insulting, that's what it is. They're not lumping me in with the rest of 'em. I'm the type that has to keep going. The type that dies with her boots on. You take my job away, that's it. Fini. The end." She drew her finger across her throat. "I got to keep moving to stay alive."

The sound of running water came from a room off the kitchen. "That means he's up and at 'em," Angie said. "My husband probably hears me out here talking up a storm, and he wants to see if I finally lost my marbles and I'm talking to myself."

Fex didn't have much time. He had to get it off his chest before Angie's husband came out for his breakfast.

"Angie, I've got this friend," he began.

She nodded. "The same one can't resist the double-dare?" she asked.

"Yeah. The same one." Fex chose his words with care. "Anyway, this kid did a jerky thing. He has a friend. A girl. He likes her a lot. They're good friends. You know, nothing romantic, just friends."

"That's good," Angie said. "Kids your age should have lots of friends, both sexes. Makes for a good time."

"Anyway," Fex went on, "this kid decides he's going to put the moves on this girl. Just to see what it's like. Only he doesn't tell her, ask her or anything. He just goes ahead. And she gets mad."

"What's this 'put the moves on' mean?" Angie said. "You mean like he's gonna make a pass?"

"Yeah. A pass. He tries to kiss her."

Angie nodded. "That's a pass, all right. No matter what they call it, it all boils down to the same thing."

Fex could hear Angie's husband opening and closing drawers in the bedroom.

"Anyway, this girl gets mad and she tells the kid he must be cuckoo. What I want to know is, what does the kid do to make friends again with the girl?"

"Well, I think he oughta tell her he's sorry. I mean"— Angie studied his face—"he shouldn't have done that. He had no right. Right? But boys been trying to kiss girls as long as I been around. Probably before too. Sometimes girls like to be kissed. Other times they figure it's not the right time yet. But this kid didn't mean any harm. If this girl's really a friend," Angie said, very serious, "it'll be all right. She'll understand. And maybe next time your friend gets the urge to put the moves on a girl, just to see what all the fuss is about, why, maybe he oughta find some older

89

girl, somebody who's ready, who knows the score. Know what I mean? That way she doesn't get sore, and your friend, maybe he picks up a coupla pointers along the way. A little practice never hurt anybody."

"Thanks a lot." Fex jumped up. He felt he couldn't sit still another minute. "For everything, Angie. I have to go."

"O.K. Glad you stopped by, like I said. You're a good kid, Fex." Angie put her arm around his shoulders. "You're all right. One thing before you go. I think you oughta tell your friend he shouldn't rush things. He's got lots of time. Maybe if he took it slow, it might work better."

They exchanged a long look. "I'll tell him," Fex said. "Thanks again." He raced down the stairs with a light heart.

15

WHEN HE GOT HOME, THEY WERE ALL FINISHING breakfast.

"Where've you been?" his mother asked. "I was beginning to worry."

"I left a note," Fex said.

"I know. But church must've been over long ago."

"I rode around some. Went over to see Angie."

"Help yourself to some eggs, then. And bacon. I put a plate for you in the oven so it would stay warm."

No sense in telling her he'd already had breakfast.

"Pete," his mother said, "please clear the table. Jerry, go wash your face. Pete, run those plates under cold water.

There's no time to clean up now. You can do that when we get back."

Fex waited, hoping she'd issue a couple of orders to his father, who was reading the papers, muttering occasionally under his breath about something the President had said. She did not.

It always seemed to Fex that his mother didn't need to take an office-management course. The way she managed them all right here at home gave her plenty of on-the-job training. She did just fine on her own, he thought.

The telephone rang.

"I'll get it," Pete said. "It's probably for me, anyway." He came back. "It's for you, clod," he said.

"Does he mean me?" Jerry asked.

"No, he means me." Fex went to the phone. "Hello," he said.

"I'm having a party," a gruff voice said. "Friday night."

"Who is this?" Fex asked.

"Barney. Who else? It's boy-girl. A boy-girl party." Barney waited for this news to sink in. "You're invited," he said at last.

The last boy-girl party Fex had been to had been about six years ago. When he was six. He remembered it clearly. After the birthday kid had opened the presents, they'd thrown food around for a while. Then the kid's mother brought out the cake and ice cream, which kept everybody quiet for as long as it took to eat. Then they'd all gone home. He suspected Barney had a different kind of boy-girl party in mind.

"Friday?" Fex said. "What time Friday?"

"Seven to ten." Barney lowered his voice. "But maybe my mom and her boyfriend will go to the movies. Then we can stretch it out a little, right? Who knows?" His charged laughter bounded over the wire.

"Call you back," Fex said. He wanted to think this over.

"Better make it quick. If you can't come, I'm asking somebody else. You got about two minutes to call back. Otherwise forget it. Just forget the whole thing."

"What's the hurry?"

"I hafta know now. Right away. My mom has to buy the grub, all like that."

"Who else is coming?"

"How do I know? Everybody I ask is coming, that's who. Not too many parties you get asked to where the kid's mother goes out to the movies, right?" Again Barney's laugh resounded.

"O.K. I'll get back to you right away." Fex hung up. Only last week he'd heard his parents discussing a party to which they'd been invited. "I don't like those people," his father had said. "I don't want to be under obligation to people I don't like. If we go to their house, we're obliged to have them to ours. No, let's not go." And they hadn't.

Fex didn't like Barney. Not really. He knew he should say no to his invitation. On the other hand, he wanted to go. Very much. He fought temptation, and temptation, as usual, won.

"Ma, Barney Barnes is having a party Friday night. Can I go?" She was on her way out the door, on her way to church.

"Barney Barnes?" she said, frowning. "I guess so. But I thought you didn't like him. You told me you didn't like him."

Why did she always remember things like that? Why did he have such a big mouth?

"Oh, he's O.K. He's not such a bad guy," Fex said lamely.

"Then go if you want to. As long as it's not late."

Fex waited until the car had disappeared around the corner. He called Barney to say he could come to the party. Then he dialed Audrey's number.

"Yup," Em answered. She liked to answer the phone.

"Let me speak to Audrey," Fex said. "Please."

"Who is it?" Em said. "Is this Fex?"

"Just let me speak to her, all right?"

Em put the phone down. Fex could hear it hit the floor. When she came back, she said, "She says she's out."

"She's out?" Fex said.

"Yup. She says she's out. I told her it was Fex, and she says she's out. That's what she says."

Em hung up. She had said what she had to say and that was that.

All right for you, he thought. If that's the way you want it. He went to the kitchen and took out the warm plate his mother had left in the oven for him. He was halfway through the eggs and bacon before he remembered he'd already had breakfast.

No wonder he felt sick to his stomach.

And, although it had started to rain, he got back on his bike and rode around some more. He thought about riding past Audrey's house just so he could thumb his nose at it and decided against the idea. He liked riding in the rain. It made him feel clean. He rode for a long time. By the time he got home, the rain was coming down in sheets. The car was in the driveway. They were home from church already. He pedaled into the garage and sat, dripping, until his mother opened the door and told him to come in immediately, before he caught his death.

16

HOW DO YOU CATCH YOUR DEATH? DO YOU REACH
out and grab it or does it touch you on the shoulder and
say, "Here I am "? Fex lay listening to the rain beat against
the house. It was Monday morning.

He felt old. Saturday night's wrestling match on
Audrey's couch had aged him. And the momentary lift he'd
gotten from yesterday's visit to Angie had worn off. This
was his week to shine in the principal's office.

"You awake?"

"No, I'm sleeping with my eyes open."

"I've got this ringing in my ears," Jerry said. "Maybe it's
from sleeping in this high altitude. Want to change places?"

"That ringing comes from you practicing on your machine," Fex told him. "That'd make anybody's ears ring."

"Hang on." One of Jerry's long, flat feet stuck out over the edge of the bunk, followed by the other. "I've got a neat new tune I want to try out on you."

Things were ganging up on him. Fex got out of bed fast. "Not now," he said. "It's late. If you start the week off late, you keep running out of time for the whole rest of it. It's murder when that happens."

Jerry slid to the floor and stood scratching himself. "If we didn't have Saturday and Sunday off, Monday wouldn't be so bad," he said.

"You might be right," Fex agreed.

It turned out to be a long day. Every time he rounded a corner, Fex thought he might run into Audrey. He half wanted to and half didn't. As it turned out, he didn't see her until lunch period. He heard her laughing. She was hanging out with a bunch of girls. She was telling them something. They were all laughing. He was sure they were laughing at him. Probably Audrey was giving them a blow-by-blow account of Saturday night. He went back to his home room. Ms. Arnow was at her desk.

"My heavens, Fex," she said, looking at her watch, "you're awfully early. Class doesn't start for another fifteen minutes."

"I know," he said. He sat down and read his English assignment. He read the same paragraph ten times and didn't know what he'd read.

When the last bell rang. Fex busied himself rummaging through his locker, pretending he'd lost something. Barney passed, stopped and thumped Fex on the back.

"Things are shaping up good," he said. "Pretty good. Everything's A-O.K. for Friday." He winked and went his way.

Holy smokes, Fex thought. Is this a party or a missile lift-off?

At last the halls were quiet. It was time to check in at Mr. Palinkas' place.

"Fex." It was Audrey. She must've been waiting for him. Down at the end of the hall, Harold, the janitor, swabbed down the floors.

"Hi," Fex said. "I called you yesterday."

"I know. I told Em to tell you I was out. I didn't want to talk to you."

"I've got to report to the principal's office," Fex said, edging past her. Yesterday he'd wanted to say he was sorry. Now he wasn't sure.

"I'm sorry about Saturday night," Audrey said.

His mouth dropped open. "*You're* sorry?" he said.

"Yes. I shouldn't have said you were cuckoo. You weren't. You were a jerk. No boy ever kissed me before.

How do I know what to expect? You made me look like a jerk too." Audrey was getting excited. "Why the heck didn't you let me in on what you were going to do? You shouldn't have sneaked up on me like that. That's what made me mad."

"What did you want me to do?" Now he was mad. "Hang a sign on me saying I was going to try to kiss you? What kind of a turkey do you take me for?"

And because he was afraid she might tell him, he escaped, running down the hall toward Mr. Palinkas' office.

"Slow down, bud!" Harold hollered. "Time for you to be outa here anyway. Clear out. No damn sense cleaning up when they're gonna get dirty tomorrow. No damn sense at all." Harold was not a cheerful man.

Fex knocked on Mr. Palinkas' door.

"Yes?" a voice said.

When he opened the door, Mr. Palinkas looked at him over the top of his glasses as if they were total strangers.

"Yes?" he said again.

"It's me, sir. Fex O'Toole." Still Mr. Palinkas looked blank. "Oh, yes," he finally said. "Mrs. Timmons is waiting for you." He turned back to his work. Feeling a strange disappointment that Mr. Palinkas didn't remember him, Fex tapped on Mrs. Timmons' door.

"Hello, Fex," she said. At least *she* remembered him. "You're right on the button. Terrible day, isn't it? I'd like you to mimeograph these fliers for me. You know how to operate the machine?" He said he did.

"O.K. Make fifty copies, please. Then see if you can locate Harold and ask him where he keeps the masking tape."

Fex made fifty copies announcing the book fair to be held June 7 and 8. Donations gladly accepted. Each sheet fell with a slight whoosh into the bin. He liked being here, alone in a place usually jammed with people. Then he found Harold and told him what he wanted. Harold fumbled at his pockets and came up with a ring of keys. "Damn woman," Harold said. "Couldn't find her nose on her face if it wasn't for me." He shuffled to the supply closet. Fex shuffled behind. "Stay out," Harold ordered. "This here is only open to me." He was like a dog defending his territory, Fex thought.

"Tell her this is it." Harold handed him two rolls of tape. "We're out. She don't order more, we don't have more. Tell her that." He turned the key in the lock and went back to his job.

Fex wondered if Harold had a wife, children maybe. Maybe he smiled at them and said pleasant things when he was home. Perhaps he even laughed. Probably not. Harold was always the same. Sour. A terrible way to be.

Mrs. Timmons gave him a couple more chores. Rain continued to pelt against the windows. "That's it for today," she finally said. "Can I give you a lift home?"

"No, thanks. I'll walk."

"In this weather?"

"I like to walk in the rain."

"I used to," Mrs. Timmons said. "Now I'm afraid I'll get pneumonia. That's the difference between being young and being old. See you tomorrow. Thanks, Fex."

Fex started home. A battered Chevy drew up beside him. The door swung open. "Get in," the driver said. Fex thought maybe he was being kidnapped and did not resent the idea.

"Tell me where you live." It was Mr. Palinkas. "I'll drop you off." Fex would rather have walked. He got in and sat very straight on the seat. Water oozed from him. The wipers made a terrific racket. Mr. Palinkas crouched over the wheel like a racing driver waiting for the starting gun. They stopped at a light.

"You may think this car looks old," Mr. Palinkas said, not taking his eyes from the red light. "But she's got life in her yet. My wife wants me to turn her in on a new one. But I figure she's been good to me. I'll be good to her." For a minute Fex wasn't sure whether he was talking about his wife or his car.

The light changed and they bounded forward. "That's my street there." Fex pointed. "You can let me out at the corner."

Mr. Palinkas drove blithely by Fex's corner. "Sit tight. I have one stop to make, then I'll drive you to your door. Don't want your mother to worry. A little weather never hurt anyone, but I know mothers. Mine worried when it was clear, worried when it rained. A champion worrier, my mother." The Chevy turned into the parking lot. Mr. Palinkas maneuvered it into a parking space as if it were a BMW or a Mercedes and he wanted to protect it from scratches. He turned off the ignition.

"The thing I remember best about my mother," he went on, "is how glad she always was to see me. She always smiled when she saw me coming. She's been dead almost ten years. There's not a day goes by that I don't think of her."

He got out. Fex watched him slosh through the rain. I didn't know he had a mother, Fex thought. He slid behind the wheel. What was it Pete had said? Your sex life begins when you have wheels? Something like that. Fex turned to see how his date was shaping up. Pretty good. Her red high-heeled shoes matched her tight-fitting red sweater. Her jeans looked as if they'd been dry-cleaned instead of washed. Cool.

"You want to go to the flicks?" Fex suggested. "Or maybe stop in at Buzzie's for a brew?"

She'd opened her beautiful red mouth to answer when the car door opened and Mr. Palinkas peered in. Fex felt the blood stain his cheeks. He slid over to his side. The walking stick was on the seat. Fex picked it up and held it on his lap.

"They had a special on Mallomars," Mr. Palinkas said, tossing a package on the back seat. "I bought six boxes. Never could get enough Mallomars." He started the engine. "Soon enough you'll be able to drive," he said.

Fex wouldn't have minded a Mallomar himself. Mr. Palinkas didn't offer him one.

"That's my house, the yellow one," Fex said.

Mr. Palinkas pulled up to the curb. "Nice house," he said. "Good place to grow up in. You're very lucky."

"Thanks for the ride." Fex handed over the stick. He'd never thought about his house being a nice one to grow up in. But it was.

"That was my mother's stick," Mr. Palinkas said, running his hands over its length. "Only thing I have that was hers." Fex opened the car door.

"Sometime, when you have a minute," Mr. Palinkas said casually, "I'd like to know what you think about."

"Think about?" Fex said stupidly.

The principal nodded. Fex closed the door and watched as Mr. Palinkas peeled out and disappeared around the corner. Then he went inside and hung his slicker on a hook in the kitchen. "Mom," he called, "you home?"

"In here," she called from the living room. "Be there in a

minute." Fex got himself a glass of milk and stood, dripping on the floor as he drank it.

"You better put on some dry clothing. Where were you?" his mother said. "I worked at the hospital today and stopped at school to pick you up but you were already gone."

"Got a ride with Mr. Palinkas."

"Oh? That was nice of him, all things considered. He strikes me as being a very compassionate man," she said.

Compassionate? Fex knew if he said, "What's that mean?" she'd tell him to look it up. He didn't feel like looking it up right at that moment, so he didn't ask.

He went upstairs to change. Did compassionate have anything to do with passionate? Passion. He tried to imagine Mr. Palinkas blowing in his wife's ear, giving her a French kiss when he got home from school. And failed.

And yet he figured compassionate and passionate must be related. Leaving his wet clothes in a heap on the floor, he went downstairs to the dictionary. He could hear his mother attacking her typewriter in her room. She was taking a typing course at the high school at night. She typed like a madwoman and made a lot of mistakes. Mr. O'Toole told her to start slowly and work up to the speed, but she didn't listen.

He turned to the C's and found compassionate. An adjective. Having or showing compassion. O.K. Compassion. A noun. A feeling of deep sympathy and sorrow for another who is stricken by suffering or misfortune accompanied by a strong desire to alleviate the pain or remove its cause.

Trust those guys who put the dictionary together, Fex thought. They nail you every time. They managed to give a definition for one word by always dragging in another word you didn't know, couldn't possibly know, the meaning of. But he'd be darned if he'd be trapped into looking up "alleviate." He could figure it out if he tried.

17

IT WAS WEDNESDAY, THE THIRD DAY OF THE monsoon. The perpetual drumming of the rain was beginning to take its toll. Tempers were short. Normally calm teachers raised their voices. Less calm teachers shouted. Kids tripped their best friends, picked fights in the hall going to and from classes, threw sandwiches at each other in the lunchroom as if they were having snowball fights. The sweetest-tempered became testy.

Of them all, only Harold improved. The more it rained, the less sour he became. He whistled as he pushed his mop. He lifted his lip in what might have been a smile. It might also have been a sneer. With Harold it was hard to tell.

Mr. Palinkas had to go out of town for two days to attend a conference on education.

"He has to make a speech," Mrs. Timmons told Fex. "He's nervous about it. Hope all goes well."

Nervous? Mr. Palinkas nervous? Fex was amazed. The idea that adults often got nervous about the same kinds of things kids did was new to him. Last fall Fex's English teacher had decided everyone should write and deliver a speech. The topic could be anything each kid chose.

"It's been my experience," the teacher told the class, "that a short speech is better than a long one. Long speeches tend to bore people. And the one thing a speaker doesn't want to do is bore the audience. So keep it short."

Fex's speech had been the shortest of all. It was an election year and he'd listened to more political speeches than he liked to remember.

"I stand before you today," he said, "with a humble heart. If nominated, I will not serve. If elected, I will not run. Thank you from the bottom of my heart. You are what makes this country great." Then he sat down. They applauded him wildly. He had to stand up and take a bow. The sound of the applause was heady stuff. He hoped Mr. Palinkas would keep his speech short. And that they gave him a standing ovation when he'd finished. A standing ovation sounded so classy, he thought.

He hadn't seen Audrey again. Not to speak to, anyway.

He'd seen her from a distance. Just as well. Barney was in high gear, talking endlessly about the coming party. Standing in the lunch line on Thursday, Fex heard a girl say, "You going to the party Friday night, Aud?"

"I guess so," he heard Audrey answer. "I said I would. Now I'm not sure I want to."

What'd she mean by that? Probably she didn't want to go now because she knew Fex was going and she didn't want to see him.

On Thursday afternoon the sky lightened. After the final bell Fex reported to the office. "Mr. Palinkas back yet?" he said.

"Not yet," Mrs. Timmons said. "Tomorrow. I must say, Fex, I'll be sorry to see you go. I've enjoyed having you here. But I know you'll be glad to have it behind you."

"I didn't mind," Fex said truthfully. "It wasn't bad. If it'd been sunny and I was missing out on a lot of stuff outside, it would've been a lot worse."

Mrs. Timmons smiled at him. She was a nice woman. He liked her.

"Don't let them get you down, Fex. Stand up for what you think is right. Don't let yourself be pushed around." She reached absentmindedly into her hair. Her pencil wasn't there.

"Oh, my word," she said. "I'm like a nut without that pencil." She darted into her office and came back with the pencil sticking behind her ear. "We all have our peculiarities," she said. "Our security blankets. This is mine."

"Like Mr. Palinkas and his walking stick," Fex said.

She looked surprised. "Yes, I suppose so. Would you mind going to the supply closet and asking Harold for some yellow lined paper? We're about out."

"Sure." Fex saw Harold pushing his mop at the end of the hall. Harold's back was turned. From where he stood, Fex couldn't tell what kind of mood Harold was in. He approached quietly, carefully.

"I need some yellow lined paper for Mrs. Timmons," he said. Harold jumped.

"It's one damn thing after another," Harold snapped. "I got better things to do than keep unlocking, locking that closet."

The real Harold was back. Sour as ever. Fex was relieved. Tomorrow, he felt sure, the rain would end.

"Fine weather for ducks," Angie said when he stopped in to see her on his way home. "You want some tea?"

"Not today, thanks," Fex said. "I have to get home. Just wanted to say hello."

"When I didn't see you yesterday, the day before even," Angie said, "I thought maybe my pancakes mighta knocked you off. They been known to do that." She laughed. "My husband said why didn't I keep you around till he got up so's he could meet you. Maybe next time, all right?"

"Sure. I'd like to meet him."

A woman came in and asked for a package of envelopes. Angie asked Fex if he'd go to the back of the store and find them for her. "I'm kinda pooped today," she said. "Haven't got my old getup and go." She pulled at the waistband of her khaki pants. "I'm not getting any fatter, that's for sure," she said. "My husband says if he can't talk me into going to Florida soon, he won't be able to see my shadow." She ran her fingers through her hair. "What's new with you?" she said.

"Well, I'm going to a party tomorrow night," Fex said. "A boy-girl party."

Angie raised her eyebrows. "No kidding? Maybe your friend can give you a couple of tips on parties before you go."

"My friend?" Fex said, forgetting.

"Yeah. You know. The one you tell me about all the time. The one has the trouble with the double-dares, the girls, all that." Fex met her eye and they both laughed.

"Have a good time," Angie said when Fex left. "Stop in and tell me about the party. I want to hear all about it."

"I will," he said. "I promise."

18

SURE ENOUGH, ON FRIDAY MORNING A COUPLE OF patches of blue sky showed themselves, proving they'd been there all along. Mr. Soderstrom called to remind Fex of his promise to look after Charlie on Saturday.

"Thought I'd get you before you took off for school," he roared from next door. Mr. Soderstrom always roared over the phone, as if he were calling from Zanzibar and had a bad connection.

"Don't forget tomorrow, Fex!" he shouted. "Ten A.M. sharp, if that's all right with you. Mrs. S. says we need two hours to reach New London. I don't agree, but women like to have their own way. Mrs. S. says we need time to get lost. We always do get lost on the road, no matter what.

She may be right. Ten it is. Does that suit you?"

"Sure," Fex agreed. "That's fine."

As he rode through the puddles on his way to school, the sun came out and rode with him on top of his head like a small, warm hat. And rested pleasantly on the backs of his hands. It felt good. Maybe by tomorrow the river would have gone down enough so that he and Charlie could go fishing.

When Fex reported to the principal's office Friday afternoon, Mr. Palinkas was at his desk. "Hello," he said to Fex, "you still here?"

"It's my last day. How was your speech?"

Mr. Palinkas looked surprised. "Speech. Oh, yes. It went rather well. How did you know I was giving a speech?"

Fex felt himself blush. "Mrs. Timmons told me." He left out what she'd said about Mr. Palinkas being nervous. He might not want anyone to know that.

"Stop by when you're through. I'd like to talk to you for a minute." Mr. Palinkas turned back to his work.

"Yes, sir." Fex was pleased. He hadn't forgotten. He'd been thinking about what Mr. Palinkas had said. No one else had ever asked him what he thought about. He wasn't sure his mother or father even cared. Sometimes his father was too busy making a living and paying the bills, and his mother was all wrapped up in her exams and making her house run as efficiently as an office.

How about them? Did he wonder what they thought about? The question amazed him. The answer was no. Maybe he should spend a little time thinking about the other guy.

Take Mrs. Timmons. Fex studied her through narrowed lids. What did she plan for herself? After she retired, was she going to sit home and darn socks? Or take care of her grandchild? Maybe she planned to take a freighter around the world, climb the Himalayas, take a boat down a fjord, eat raw octopus in the Far East. It was entirely possible.

Mrs. Timmons sighed and worried her pencil around in her hair as if she had an elusive itch and were trying to pin it down.

"I'll miss you, Fex," she said. "You've been a great help. Stop by and visit now and then, will you?"

Fex promised he would. He went to Mr. Palinkas' office and stood at the door, waiting. Mr. Palinkas lifted his head and stared. Then he blinked. "What can I do for you?" he said.

"You said to stop by when I was through." Fex began to stutter. "You—you said to . . ."

Mr. Palinkas' face cleared. "You're right." He pushed the pile of papers in front of him to one side.

"So," he said. "You've finished your sentence and you're getting out of the hoosegow, eh?"

"What?" Fex said stupidly.

"Hoosegow. Jail. Old-fashioned slang for jail."

"Oh. Yeah. Well, I wanted to say good-bye." Mr. Palinkas hadn't remembered after all. He wasn't really interested in Fex's thoughts. People always pretended to be interested when they weren't.

"Have you thought about what I said?" Mr. Palinkas asked suddenly. "I asked you to tell me what you thought about if you felt like it."

Fex smiled back at him. "Yeah, I've thought some. A little."

"Sit down," Mr. Palinkas said. Fex sat boldly in a chair facing him. He folded his hands primly, like a lady riding a bus, looking out the window. He met Mr. Palinkas' eye.

"I think I'd like to change everything about myself," he said. "Get a new skin, everything. I'd like to be a winner."

Mr. Palinkas sighed. "Wouldn't we all?" he said.

"I wonder sometimes if I'm really an O'Toole or if maybe somebody stole me from the hospital and changed my name. I don't look like anyone else in my family and sometimes I don't feel like a member of my family," Fex said in a rush. Now that he'd started, he couldn't seem to stop.

Mr. Palinkas nodded. "I remember that feeling," he said.

"I think about being a hero. About being famous. And rich," Fex continued. "If ever I was rich, I would do something for my parents. Like maybe buy them a house with a swimming pool. No," he corrected himself, "my father wouldn't like a swimming pool. He says they're too much trouble. But I'd treat them to an ocean voyage. My mother is always talking about going on an ocean voyage. She says she'd sit in a deck chair and watch the ocean go by and eat caviar."

Mr. Palinkas smiled. "That sounds good," he said.

"Me and my older brother aren't friends," Fex said. "We don't like each other much." ·

"That happens," Mr. Palinkas said. "More often than you think."

"But Jerry and me—Jerry's my younger brother, he plays the violin, and we sleep in bunk beds. Jerry's my friend. I like him. Maybe I love him." Fex stopped, astounded at himself, saying these private things aloud.

"My father gets very mad at me lots of times," he went on. "He gets furious. He shouts at me when I do dumb things. When I do things kids double-dare me to. He says I behave like a fool."

"And do you?"

"Sometimes."

I talk too much, Fex thought. He wished he could take back some of the things he'd said.

Mr. Palinkas said, "You remind me of myself when I was your age."

"I do?"

"Yes. It's somewhat reassuring to know that boys haven't changed as much as they'd have you believe they have."

The telephone rang on Mr. Palinkas' desk. He picked it up. Fex nodded good-bye and left.

Tonight was Barney's party. Tonight was the big night.

19

THIS TIME JERRY WATCHED FEX COMB HIS HAIR IN front of the mirror.

"What's happening?" he said.

"Nothing." Fex went on combing. He would've used the bathroom but Pete was monopolizing it, as usual.

"You never comb your hair at night," Jerry said accusingly.

"I'm going to a party."

Jerry sat up. "With girls. A boy-girl party. If you comb your hair, it must be a boy-girl party."

"Yeah," Fex drawled, acting as if he went to one of those every day.

"Do you kiss girls when you go to those parties?" Jerry asked.

"How do I know? The last time I went to a boy-girl party I was only a little kid. All we did was eat and throw stuff around the dining room," Fex said, pulling on his sweater.

"Did you ever kiss a girl, Fex?" Jerry asked.

Under his sweater Fex felt himself blush.

"No," he said, coming up for air. "Why?"

"I just wondered when you were supposed to start, that's all." Jerry rested his chin in his hands and stared down at Fex, his eyes bright, his face very curious. "I figure I've got lots of time but not you. Next year you're in junior high. That's when all that junk starts."

"All what junk?" After-shave lotion or no after-shave lotion? Fex debated. He settled for slapping his cheeks vigorously, the way they did on TV commercials. That ought to do it.

"All that sexy junk. Junior high is when it starts," Jerry said, very knowing.

"Who told you?"

"I just know. I listen a lot. Even if you don't feel like it, you have to do that stuff in junior high. Kiss girls, take off your clothes, all that."

Fex's palms became clammy. "Listen," he said, "I'm having a hard enough time already without you giving me

118

advice. O.K." He gave himself a final check in the mirror. "Ready or not, here I come."

He pushed everything he'd left on the floor underneath his bunk. "Don't wait up for me, son," he said. "I'll probably be late, very late."

"Hey, Fex." When he turned, Jerry was crouched on the edge of his bunk, hanging a moon down at him. His skinny little behind glowed pale in the light.

"You look like a honeydew melon," Fex told him. "Two honeydew melons."

"Don't do anything I wouldn't do!" Jerry crowed.

"Get outa here." Fex reached up and pulled Jerry down to the floor. They wrestled there for a couple of minutes, laughing so hard Pete came out of the bathroom to see what was going on.

"What's the big joke?" he demanded.

Both boys lay on the floor looking up at their older brother. "Whoooeee!" they cried, holding their noses. "You smell!"

Pete snapped his wet towel at them, but his heart wasn't in it. He looked down at Jerry. "What's he doing flashing his bare butt around?" he asked crossly.

"Telling me the facts of life," Fex said. He and Jerry rolled around a little while longer. Then Fex got up and pulled himself together. "I have to go," he said. "The chicks are waiting." Jerry jumped up, pulling on his pants. He did a little dance.

"You guys are a couple of nerds," Pete said. "When I have the time, I might sit you down and give you the benefit of my experience. Let you have the straight scoop, about sex and . . ."

"And what?" Mr. O'Toole stood in the doorway.

"Oh, hi, Dad," Pete said. "What's up?"

"I was just going to ask you that. From the noise up here, I thought the ceiling might be coming down."

"It was them," Pete said. "They were horsing around. I didn't do anything."

Mr. O'Toole looked at Fex. "I thought you were going to Barney's party," he said. "I was going to ask you what time I'm supposed to pick you up."

"Pick me up?" Fex tugged at his clothes, brushed himself off.

"You look as if you'd been in a fight," his father said. "If you're going to a party, better clean yourself up." He turned and started down the stairs.

"Dad." Fex went after him. "You don't have to pick me up. I can walk home."

"What time is it over?"

"Oh, about ten, I guess," Fex said airily.

"I'll settle for nine," Mr. O'Toole said.

"Dad, I'm not a baby. I'm almost twelve."

"Nine-thirty. You call me when it's over and I'll meet you on the corner so they won't know your old man came for you. How's that?" His father smiled at Fex.

"Thanks, Dad." Fex went back to his room and combed his hair some more.

"I'm staying awake until you get home," Jerry said. "Tell me all about it, O.K.?"

"If I live to tell the tale," Fex said. "I just wonder if going to a party is worth all this trouble."

"Probably not," Jerry said, taking up his violin. Fex fled.

20

BARNEY LIVED UP BY THE HOSPITAL. IN A PALE
brown apartment house at the top of the hill. Barney's
mother was a nurse. Every Monday morning Barney told
tales of the goings-on in the emergency room over the
weekend. He said the weekend was when things really
started hopping. Especially if there was a full moon. You
wouldn't believe what went on there Saturday nights if
there was a full moon, Barney said.

"Let me out on the corner, Dad," Fex told his father. "I'll
walk the rest of the way."

He didn't want to be the last one at the party. It was
almost seven. On the other hand, he also didn't want to be
the first. He didn't know which was worse. After his father

let him off, he dawdled, taking his time, walking slowly, keeping an eye on the entrance to the emergency room. He'd been there a couple of times himself. Once when he'd broken his collarbone, another time when they'd thought he might have appendicitis. It turned out to be only a bad stomachache.

It seemed to Fex as he rang Barney's bell that he could hear party sounds coming from above. He waited for Barney to buzz so he could open the door. The hall smelled damp and musty and of various kinds of food. Barney leaned over the stairwell, watching him come. His face looked very wide and flat from this angle. He didn't speak. Just suspended himself and watched without saying a word. Fex trudged up the stairs, head down, already sorry he'd come.

"You're the first," Barney hissed as Fex reached his floor. Fex's heart sank.

"Hello!" a blond woman wearing a pale blue pants suit greeted him. "I'm Barney's mom." She smiled without showing her teeth.

"I'm Fex O'Toole," Fex said. He put out his hand. She shook it.

"Oh, Barn's told me all about you," she said. She seemed glad to meet him. "I like to hear about Barn's friends."

"How are you, Mrs. Barnes?" Fex said. He looked past her into the living room. It was empty.

Barney jabbed him in the ribs. "Her name's not Mrs. Barnes," he said. A man came out of the bedroom. He, too, wore a pale blue pants suit.

"This is Dougie," Barney said. "Meet Fex O'Toole, Dougie." Dougie rattled when he walked, due to all the gold chains he wore around his neck. His hair was thin and so artfully arranged over his scalp that it looked like the tributaries of a river marked on a map. He also smiled without revealing his teeth. It was uncanny. They must practice smiling that way, Fex thought. He didn't think it would be easy.

"Hey," Dougie said, "how's it going?" He and Barney's mother went into the kitchen. There was a sound of scuffling. "Dougie!" Barney's mother cried out. "Stop that! Not now!" Fex and Barney stood in the middle of the rug, looking at their feet. Probably the guy was blowing in her ear, Fex thought.

"That's the boyfriend," Barney whispered unnecessarily. Fex had already figured that out. "The one that gets the Mopeds wholesale."

"Oh," Fex said. "Yeah." The silence stretched out, into the corners of the room. Fex prayed for the bell downstairs to ring, for lots of kids to arrive. A wailing ambulance pulled up beneath the window. Barney raced to look out. Fex followed.

"This way I keep tabs on everything," Barney said. They

looked out and saw nothing but the ambulance, its lights flashing.

The bell finally rang. Barney buzzed in the guests. Fex stood quietly, not sure of what to do, where to go. Barney's mom and Dougie bustled back and forth, carrying bowls of potato chips, Fritos, pretzels.

"Pretty good feed, eh?" Dougie said, slapping Fex on the back. With a flourish he brought forth an ice bucket filled to the top with ice cubes.

"Nothing but the soft stuff for you kids, though," he said, smiling his peculiar smile. "Be a couple of years before you try the hard stuff, right? You want to hold off on that for a long time. Not good to start too early, I say. Bad for the body. You want to take care of the body, the muscles. Take regular exercise. Now you take me. A hundred pushups at night, a hundred in the morning. Work out at the gym regular. Look at that." In a flash he'd rolled up his pale blue sleeve to show Fex his muscles.

"All right," Fex said as he watched Dougie's muscles ripple. The room began to fill up. Fex didn't see Audrey. He was afraid Dougie might not let him loose, might keep him there all night, showing off his muscles.

Maybe Audrey had decided not to come. He wouldn't be too surprised at that. Someone put on a record. Kids started to dance, throwing their arms up in the air as if they were trying to get rid of them. Miraculously, Dougie disappeared. Fex went over to where the soda was laid out and helped himself to a Coke. He filled up a glass with ice and poured in the Coke slowly. Then he leaned against the door and watched the dancers. Fex wasn't sure he liked parties. He liked the idea of them, but the actual party itself he wasn't too sure about.

"Hey, Fex!" Barney hollered. "Come on and dance!" He gyrated by with a girl Fex had never seen before. She was tall, with long brown hair. Her jeans fit her as if they'd been pasted on. She was older than he, fourteen, maybe fifteen. But still in good shape. She was beautiful.

Fex stared at her as she danced by, tossing her hair like a girl in a shampoo commercial. Then he saw Audrey talking to a couple of kids from school. She didn't look at him. I bet she knows I'm here, he thought. I just bet she does, and she won't even say hello.

Someone shoved him hard in the middle of his back. "Long time no see," a voice said. Fex turned and looked up, way up, at Wesley. Wesley was the kid who'd double-dared him to ride his bike up on the parkway last year. Wesley had gone to private school this year. Wesley was a troublemaker.

"How'd you get so tall?" Fex asked him. He was amazed at how much Wesley had grown. Wesley stuck out his foot. Against his will, Fex was impressed. Wesley wore the most terrific-looking pair of cowboy boots Fex had ever seen.

They were smooth and glossy, with high slanted heels. The real McCoy. No wonder Wesley looked so tall.

"You fall down much?" Fex asked, jealous of Wesley's heels.

Wesley got red in the face. "You still up to your ass in double-dares?" he said, snuffling juicily at his own wit.

"Wesley, the worm," Fex said. He stood and watched the dancers, who looked like whirling dervishes, all elbows and arms and legs. He craned his neck, looking for Barney and his partner. No luck. Boy, if Pete ever caught a glimmer of Wesley's boots, Fex thought, he'd flip. Flip right out. Ever since a girl had told Pete he reminded her of Robert Redford, he hadn't stopped talking about buying a pair of cowboy boots. Fex finished his Coke and debated about having another. Dougie and Barney's mom were nowhere in sight. Maybe they'd already gone to the movies.

Then he caught sight of Barney, all by himself.

"Who's she?" Fex asked. "The girl you were dancing with. I never saw her before."

"Ain't she something?" Barney said. "Her mother and my mother are friends. She's really built, huh?"

"What's her name?"

"Tara."

"Tara? I never heard of a name like that."

"Isn't it cool? Her mother named her after Scarlett

O'Hara's house. In *Gone With the Wind*. She was watching a rerun of *Gone With the Wind* when she went into labor. That's why she called the kid Tara."

Barney's mother beckoned to him. Fex saw her whisper something in Barney's ear. He saw Barney nodding. The music went on and on. Fex wanted to dance, but everyone he knew was already dancing. Audrey was nowhere in sight. There was hardly any room to move, the room was so crowded.

"My mom is slipping out with Dougie. They're going to the tavern to see some friends," Barney said. He smiled. "I guess now's the time for some action, huh?" Fex watched as Barney's mom and Dougie went out the door. He heard Barney's mom tell him to be sure to lock up behind them. It didn't pay to be careless, she said.

The minute they'd gone, Barney sauntered over to where Fex stood. "Whadya say? Think it's time to turn off the lights?"

At that moment the music stopped. Tara and Wesley had been dancing together. They came to a halt directly in front of Fex. He noticed that Wesley was almost as tall as Tara. With his boots on, that is. Tara went to sit down on the couch. She lifted her hair off her neck to cool it. Someone brought her a glass of ginger ale.

"Give her a smooch or two, why don'tcha?" Barney

spoke into Fex's ear. "She's been around. She knows the ropes, I bet."

"Don't be a jerk," Fex said. A shiver ran down his spine. He remembered what Angie had said. About finding an older girl, someone who knew the ropes, to practice on. There she was.

"I double-dare you, Fexy," Barney whispered. "Now's your chance. I double-dare you to put the moves on that Tara chick."

Fex felt his ears getting red. His feet sweated.

"Put another record on!" someone hollered.

"Put the lights out!" another voice cried.

Fex could feel Barney watching him. Why not? He'd probably never have another chance like this. He went over and sat down beside Tara. Barney moved toward the light switch.

"Hello," he said. "My name is Fex. I never heard of *Gone With the Wind*, but I think Tara is a nice name." It was the most incredibly dumb thing to say. Tara turned her cool blue eyes on him. She looked at him as if he were crazy. Maybe he was. She had on some sort of fuzzy sweater. Up close she seemed to him as beautiful as Jodie Foster. Or Brooke Shields. He smiled at her and the lights went out.

"I want my mother!" a voice across the room cried out,

followed by a burst of laughter. Fex lunged, touched something soft. He grabbed whatever it was and held on.

Fex put his mouth where he thought her mouth should be. He felt the smooth skin of her face, her eyelashes batting at his cheeks like a moth held captive in a jar.

The lights went on.

"Hey, hey," Wesley shouted, standing near the light switch. "Looka that!" All eyes were on Fex.

He was practically sitting in Tara's lap. His head was resting on her sweater. In the middle. In the middle of where her breasts were. The girls he knew didn't have breasts. But she did. His hand was on her jeans.

"What is this?" Tara's voice was strident, reached to the four corners of the room. She stood up and dumped him on the floor. As if he'd been an overfriendly and unwelcome dog. A wave of laughter swelled and broke over Fex's head. From where he lay he could see Wesley and Barney pounding one another on the back, laughing so hard saliva ran down their chins. He saw Audrey, her face pale, her dark eyes huge. She looked as if she were about to cry.

Music began. The group around him broke up. Someone started to dance. Fex got up. Like a sleepwalker, he made his way to the door.

He tried to let himself out of the apartment, but the lock on the door was so complicated he had to go looking for Barney. Luckily, he wasn't far away.

Fex went up to him and said, "Let me out. I'm going home and I can't unlock the door." Without a word, Barney did as Fex asked. The stairs seemed endless. Fex's feet felt as if they were too big, too heavy for his body. Each step was an effort. He was almost on the ground floor when he heard running steps behind him. If it's one of those guys, Fex thought, Wesley or Barney, I'll kill 'em.

It was Audrey.

"You all right?" she asked.

Her concern infuriated him. "You're always asking me that," he snapped. "Sure I'm all right."

"I can't believe you keep this up," she said. "When are you going to stop being the fall guy?" Her voice had gone from soft to hard. "He double-dared you, right? To kiss her? A girl you never even met before. How dumb can you get?"

He wanted to cry, wanted to hit her. And did neither. "Just let me alone," he said.

"What are you trying to prove, Fex?" she said.

"Nothing. I'm not trying to prove anything. Just let me alone. It's none of your business anyway."

"You're right. It isn't any of my business. Except I thought we were friends. I also thought you were smart. But you act like such a jerk I must've been wrong."

Because she had hurt him, he wanted to hurt her in return. "What makes you think somebody double-dared me?" He looked at her. "That Tara's really something. I wanted to kiss her. That's why I did. I just plain wanted to. So what's wrong with that?"

He left her standing in the lobby and went out into the street. The fresh air felt good against his face. He decided to walk home. It was too early for his father to pick him up. As he went down the hill, the ambulance passed him, siren sounding, lights flashing. And there wasn't even a full moon, Fex thought.

He ran most of the way home. It was farther than he'd thought. When he came in the front door, his father looked at his watch.

"I was just about to go for you," he said. "You're home early."

"Yeah," Fex said. "It wasn't such a hot party. It was sort of a drag, as a matter of fact. So I decided to split early."

"Oh?" his father said. "Well, that's the luck of the draw. You win some, you lose some."

"I guess," Fex said. "Think I'll hit the sack, Dad. Good night."

"Good night, Fex," his father said.

Upstairs, Jerry was waiting for him. "Mom told me about a hundred times to turn off the light," he chortled. "But every time she went back down, I turned it on again. How was it?"

Fex took off his sweater and shirt and put them neatly

away in his drawer. Then he sat down on the side of his bunk and removed his shoes and socks. His feet smelled. Good. He was glad his feet smelled.

"It was O.K.," he said.

"How about the kissing?" Jerry said. "You get to kiss anybody, Fex?"

"Oh, shut up and go to sleep." Fex felt as if he hadn't slept in days.

"What's eating you?" Jerry gazed down on Fex with a hurt expression. "What happened?"

"I don't want to talk about it," Fex said. He turned out the light and stared into the blackness. Angie, he thought, you gave me a bum steer. You said to find somebody older, somebody who knows the score. That's just what I did. I found her, all right. Tara was perfect. But look what happened. Just look. And although he was exhausted, it seemed hours before he finally fell asleep.

21

FEX WOKE ON SATURDAY, STILL WEAK WITH SHAME.
He lay flat on his belly, his face smashed into the bed-
clothes, and wished he could smother himself in them and
never get up and face the world.

With horrible clarity he remembered Tara's face when
the lights had gone on, how she'd sounded when she spat
out, "What is this?"

But then he smelled bacon cooking, and that made things
better. Funny how the smell of bacon cooking always did.
Bacon was the only thing he could think of that lived up to
its promise. Even roast beef didn't, he thought.

From the stillness in the room, he knew that Jerry had
left. Left him alone. Why not? He'd been snotty to Jerry

last night, acting as if what had happened had been his fault. He'd try to make it up to him. How he didn't know, but he'd try. Jerry was a good kid and didn't deserve the treatment he'd gotten.

When he went downstairs, the rest had gone. Except for his mother. "Mom, I'm sitting for Charlie today," Fex said. "All day. They're going to a wedding."

"Dad said you came home early last night. Everything all right? Was it fun?" His mother had been taking a bath when he got in.

"Fine," Fex said. "It was fine." Why did everyone ask him if everything was all right, if he was all right? He must look like a first-class wimp. Wimpy O'Toole, they'd call him in later life. Fex would be forgotten.

He stared at his mother. Her face was shiny, her hair untidy. Suddenly he thought of something Mr. Palinkas had said. "Mom," Fex said, "are you glad to see me?"

She looked surprised. "Now, you mean?" she asked.

"No, I mean are you always glad to see me? When I come home from school, when I come down for breakfast, all the time." He studied her face. He would know if she lied to him.

"Fex." She shook her head. "Of course I am. I love you. You're my child and I love you." She smiled at him across the table but didn't touch him. Which was a good thing. He didn't want her to touch him. He only wanted to know the answer. She was telling him the truth. He could tell.

"I'm off," he said. "If you want me I'm at Soderstroms'."

Mr. Soderstrom was standing on the stoop, watch in hand, when Fex arrived. "Good boy!" he shouted. "Right on time! For all her talk about ten-sharp departure, Mrs. S. is still in her boudoir, getting herself doozied up for the event. You know women. I can get myself together in a trice but it takes Mrs. S. a trifle longer. Oh, a trifle longer."

Mr. Soderstrom was resplendent in a navy blue blazer with brass buttons, gray flannel slacks, and white shoes. One thing about having such a big beard, Fex thought, was that for all anyone knew, he could have on a dirty shirt and no tie underneath that beard. No one would be the wiser.

"You're pretty doozied up yourself," Fex told him.

Mr. Soderstrom looked pleased. "I dress for the occasion," he said grandly. "Keep up appearances."

Fex asked where Charlie was hiding.

"Out in the sandbox, running a small war. Waiting for you. Bought him a fishing rod. Thought you might take him fishing. He'd like that. Watch the river, though, Fex. Keep an eye on him. Oh, there you are, my dear." Mr. Soderstrom beamed. "You look ravishing, simply ravishing. Put all the other ladies to shame, won't she?" he asked Fex.

Fex smiled, not knowing what to say. He settled on, "Hello, Mrs. Soderstrom."

She narrowed her eyes and looked at him from across the

room. She needed glasses, Fex figured. His grandmother looked like that when she was too vain to wear her glasses.

"Fex?" Mrs. Soderstrom said. She wasn't sure who he was.

"Yes, ma'am," he replied, sounding like some phony hoked-up cowboy.

She didn't answer. She was too busy studying her image in the mirror.

"You don't think the earrings are too much?" she asked.

"The perfect touch!" Mr. Soderstrom exclaimed.

She smoothed her dress across her stomach and looked sideways at herself. "I've gained weight," she said in a way that indicated that she held Mr. Soderstrom directly responsible for her extra pounds.

He took her arm in a masterful fashion. "You are a vision," he said firmly. "Now let's be on our way."

Mrs. Soderstrom moistened her lips and smiled in Fex's direction. "I boiled some eggs," she said. "For egg salad sandwiches. You know how to make egg salad sandwiches?"

"Sure. Mash 'em with a fork and add mayonnaise," Fex said.

"Make sure Charlie goes to the bathroom even if he says he doesn't have to," she told Fex. "You're sure about the earrings?"

Mr. Soderstrom opened the door and gave her a gentle push toward it. "Watch the steps, my dear, with those high heels." He turned and winked at Fex. "Should be home about four, five at the latest. Take good care of the boy."

"I will." Would they never leave? "Have a good time."

He watched as Mr. Soderstrom helped his wife into the car, tucking up the hem of her dress carefully so it wouldn't get caught in the door. He treated her, Fex thought, as if she were made of something breakable. As the car pulled out, he could hear Mrs. Soderstrom giving her husband directions on where to turn, what route to take. Mrs. S. was a bossy lady, he decided. Thank God she wasn't his mother.

Shortly before eleven Fex and Charlie ate their egg salad sandwiches outside. It was sort of early for lunch but Charlie claimed he was hungry.

"Those are probably the best egg salad sandwiches you have ever eaten," Fex told Charlie. "Or ever will." Charlie smiled in agreement. He looked sleepy.

"How about a little shut-eye?" Fex suggested.

"It's still morning," Charlie said indignantly. "I don't shut eyes in the morning. I'm too old for that."

"O.K. then, I'll tell you a story."

"That would be good," Charlie said, settling in Fex's lap. Fex told him the same old tale he'd made up, about good monsters and bad monsters and the continuing battle they fought. The good monsters always won. Charlie liked that part.

When Fex finished, Charlie stayed where he was for a while, thinking things over. "I don't think it's fair," he said at last. "The way the good ones always win. That's not fair."

"O.K. Next time I'll have the bad ones win. How's that?" Fex said.

"That'd be nice," Charlie agreed. "Now let's go fishing."

They stood on the riverbank and gazed into its dark depths. The water, normally clear to the bottom, was turgid and black. They watched it bungle its angry way over the rocks, rushing, pushing its way downstream.

"I never saw it like this," Fex said. "Not ever. And I've lived here since before you were born, Charlie."

Charlie did not look impressed by this impressive statement. He squatted by the river's edge. "I can't see anything," he said. "No fish, nothing. It's too dark inside the water."

Fex squatted beside him. "Hey!" someone shouted. Fex looked up.

A gang, led by Barney, approached. "If it isn't Double-Dare O'Toole!" he cried, grinning, looking around to make sure his followers joined in the fun. "How's it going, Double-Dare O'Toole?" he shouted.

Doesn't he ever know when to quit? Fex thought.

"Come on, Charlie," Fex urged, "let's go see what's on the tube. Let's catch a couple of cartoons."

Charlie didn't stir. He stayed where he was, looking at

the big kids loping across the grass. This was fun, like a party.

Fex stood his ground. "Clear out," he said.

The mob nudged one another and laughed. "Make us," one of them said.

Fex put out his hand. If necessary, he'd drag the kid inside to safety until these guys took off. "Come on, Charlie," he said, his voice cracking. "Let's go."

"Why don't you go for a swim, Fex?" Barney said, mocking him. "Suppose I double-dare you? How about that?" He turned to his troops for approval. They gave it. "Yeah!" they cried. "Yeah! Yeah!"

"I double-dare you to go for a swim right now, O'Toole!"

Charlie stayed where he was, squatting by the water, watching, his smile as bright as ever.

"I'm not falling for any more of that crap," Fex said.

"O.K.," Barney said slowly, distinctly, "how about you, Charlie? I dare you, Charlie. You go for a swim."

Fex stepped backward, keeping Barney in his sights.

He heard Charlie say, "O.K.," heard a splash. Charlie had jumped into the boiling current. He'd been to the Y for swimming lessons. He knew what he was doing.

The water surged over his head. All Fex could see was Charlie's bright red shirt. In the dark water it stood out like a beacon. Then he saw Charlie's legs waving in the air as he was carried bouncing over the rocks.

Fex jumped in, keeping the red shirt in the center of his terrified vision. He fought the powerful rush of water as it picked him up, drove him along, down, and farther down.

The shirt. The red shirt. If you lose that, you lose Charlie, a voice screamed inside Fex's head. You lose everything. You lose Charlie. With an immense effort he kept his head up and his arms out, ready to grab and hold on. Red shirt. Red shirt. Ahead was blackness, the terrible opaque blackness of the water. It seemed to Fex that he saw a spot of color. Using his arms, his feet, his legs, his heart, he fought his way toward it. He reached out, almost had it, and then it was gone. Again he reached out, his arms and heart straining. He touched something, grabbed hold, held on. His heart was going to burst. He lifted what he'd caught, pulled, tugged, lifted again.

Then there were two men beside him, helping him. Two tremendous men. They must be giants, they were so huge. They lifted up the red spot, and it was Charlie. They carried him and Fex out of the raging current and brought them to the bank of the river.

"My God, my God!" someone said. That was all Fex heard. He was surrounded by a wall of legs. All he could see were legs. Thousands of legs. Noisy legs.

"It's all right," one of the men said. "I think we got him in time." They bent over Charlie, breathing air into his little red mouth. Fex put his head in his hands and vomited. Someone held his head.

I think we got him in time. That's what the man said. Fex looked up, dazed. He saw Barney standing on the fringe of the crowd, mouth open, eyes bugging out. He struggled to get up. He wanted to beat Barney to a pulp. His legs wouldn't support him. You've killed him, a voice in his head shouted. Barney, I'm talking to you. And then another voice said, You know you might've been killed, don't you? Only fools accept dares to do things that might result in injury or death. It was his father, talking to him, Fex.

He lay back and closed his eyes. It wasn't Barney, it was me. If Charlie had died, I would've been responsible. I'm the big hotshot double-dare guy, the guy who never turns down a double-dare. He smelled the river on himself. It was my fault, not Barney's. Never again. Injury or death. He couldn't stop crying. Or maybe it was the river water seeping out of his eyes.

"It's all right, it's all right," he heard a familiar voice murmur. Arms took him in, held him. It was his father. It was the first time in years, since he'd been very small, that he could remember his father holding him this way.

He heard someone crying. Very loudly. It was Charlie. Charlie didn't cry often. When he did, he really let go. It was a sweet sound. Fex put his head against his father's chest and closed his eyes.

22

WHEN FEX WOKE ON SUNDAY HE FELT BRUISED. AS IF he'd been in an accident. As if someone had stomped on him. It had been a rough two days. Friday night, then Saturday. No wonder he felt bruised. He went again to early church and listened to the sermon, which was about treating your neighbor as you would yourself. He put a dime in the collection plate. When church was over, he got on his bike. He figured he'd ride around a bit. He didn't want to get to Angie's too early. He wondered if she made pancakes every Sunday, if she expected him. He hoped so.

He rode past Audrey's house, crouched low over his handlebars, like a racing driver, in case Audrey looked out the window and saw him. He didn't want her to think he wanted to see her. The house looked closed, as if the family had gone on vacation. When he got to the end of her street, he turned and rode past once more, eyes straight ahead, arms folded across his chest. Look. No hands.

The streets were deserted, the morning light green and shining. Fex enjoyed the solitude, the feeling of being absolutely alone. That was a fine feeling as long as you knew you had a place to go, he thought. There was a calm, swelling sensation in his chest. He hadn't felt calm for some time. He also felt virtuous because he'd been to church already and the people inside the houses he passed were probably still in their bathrobes, drinking coffee, yawning.

He postponed riding to Angie's because he so much looked forward to going there, sitting with her, eating her good food, telling her about the party (the parts he felt like telling her), maybe having her give him a few more words of advice. He wasn't going to say, "Your plan didn't work, Angie. My friend tried putting the moves on an older girl and it didn't work." He wasn't going to say that exactly. Something like it but not exactly that. He wasn't going to blame Angie for what had happened. When he told Angie that, she'd probably raise her shoulders, throw out her hands, and say, "What're you gonna do?" the way she always did. He smiled in anticipation. Then, at the end, when he was leaving, he'd tell her about Charlie. No big deal, just tell her what happened.

The sun rose higher, hotter. He figured the time had come for him to head for Angie's. Leisurely he rode toward her house. When he arrived, he saw six or seven cars parked out front. She must be having a party, a brunch or something. There was no one around he could ask. Well, if Angie was having a party, he couldn't knock on her door. That wouldn't be right. Then she'd have to invite him in whether she wanted to or not. He was disappointed. Maybe if he came back later in the day, Angie's guests would be gone. He'd give it a try.

On his way home he rode past the general store. On the door a sign said something that looked like: CLOSED DUE TO DEATH IN THE FAMILY. Fex got off his bike and walked up close to make sure that's what the sign said. So that's why the cars were there. Angie's husband's heart must've given out at last. Poor Angie. He felt bad for her. He rode home, his heart heavy.

As he opened the door, the phone rang. When Fex picked it up, Audrey's voice said, "Angie died."

"What? Wha-wha-what did you say?" Fex stuttered the way he did when something unexpected and upsetting happened. "I was just at the store," he said. "There was a sign saying they were closed due to a death in the family. I thought it was her husband."

"My mother went to get the papers. A man said the store

wouldn't be open today. He put the sign up. He said it was Angie who died."

"When?"

"I don't know. Maybe today, maybe yesterday. They're having visiting hours tomorrow night at the Bennett Funeral Home. Tonight and tomorrow. I'm going tomorrow night."

"Who're you going to visit?" Fex asked.

"The family, dope. It's a wake. You pay your respects. I'm going tomorrow. If you want, be at my house at a quarter to seven," Audrey said.

"What'd she die of?" Fex said.

"How do I know?" Audrey sounded angry. "The man said she died suddenly. What's that supposed to mean? Does that mean all of a sudden she dropped dead? Why do they use stupid words like that when they're talking about a person? I don't understand it. I think it stinks. That's what I think," and she hung up on him. He sat looking at the humming receiver, trying to make sense out of the whole thing.

How could Angie die when it had been her husband who was sick? Only a couple of days ago Angie'd been hopping around behind the cash register in her old army pants. She wasn't even old. She wasn't even a senior citizen.

"What's the matter?" Fex's father asked.

"Angie died."

"Angie?"

"At the general store. You know her."

Fex turned away. He didn't want his father to see his face.

"I'm sorry, Fex." His father patted him on the back. "I thought you might want to see this."

He held out the Bridgeport paper. There was a picture of Fex. The caption under the picture read:

TWELVE-YEAR-OLD RESCUES TOT FROM RIVER.

There he was, puny, ugly, hair matted down, clothes sticking to him. Charlie wasn't even in the picture. If that's what I look like, Fex thought, I better crawl in a hole and stay there.

Pete came up behind him as he studied his image.

"Will you look at that?" Pete's voice was mocking, but there was something new there, something hard to recognize because it was so new. "Baby brother is a hero," Pete said. "Will wonders never cease? Old Double-Dare O'Toole is a hero."

Without warning, without planning, Fex leaped on him. Rage made him strong, and he brought Pete to the floor more easily than he ever would have dreamed possible. Through clenched teeth he said, "You ever call me that again and I'll break your head." He put his hands around Pete's throat. His father watched and made no attempt to stop him.

"Never again," Fex said, speaking slowly so Pete would remember what he said. "Never again. You hear me?"

Wordlessly, Pete nodded. He understood. Fex could tell from his eyes that he understood. Pete had never looked at him like that before. But he would again. Lots of times.

Jerry said nothing. But when Fex went to his room, their room, he found a poster Jerry had made. He had stuck it to the mirror with Scotch tape. It was a picture of him, Fex. A round face, round eyes, a smiling mouth. Over the head was a halo. Barely recognizable but a halo nevertheless. Underneath Jerry had written, FRANCIS XAVIER O'TOOLE. BROTHER AND HERO.

That kid was too much. Fex smiled in spite of himself. He heard a noise. His mother stood in the doorway.

"I'm so sorry to hear about Angie, Fex," she said. "I know you and she were friends. I know you'll miss her."

"Audrey and I are going to the funeral home tomorrow night," Fex said. "To pay our respects. Is that all right?"

She nodded. "I'm proud of you, Fex" she said. "For a number of reasons." Then she left him abruptly, before he had to answer her, which was a good thing.

Monday morning he overslept. When he came downstairs, the clock said it was after nine.

"Why don't I run you over?" his mother said.

"No, thanks. I'll ride my bike."

At school he slipped into his home room. No one looked up. They were studying the English assignment. Ms. Arnow was writing on the blackboard. She didn't pay any attention to him either. He opened his book to what he hoped was the right page. "All right, class." Ms. Arnow turned away from the blackboard. Everyone stood and sang "For He's a Jolly Good Fellow."

Fex looked at the floor. The ends of his ears tingled. He tried to look as if they were singing for somebody else. In the afternoon Ms. Arnow handed him a note asking him to come to the principal's office after school.

Oh, Lord, he thought. What now?

When he tapped on the door, Mr. Palinkas said, "Yes?" in his impatient way. Fex went in and waited. Mr. Palinkas finally looked up. "It's me, Fex O'Toole," Fex said.

"So it is," The principal got up, came around to the front of his desk, and shook Fex's hand. "Well, well," he said. "You had me worried there for a while. But now it looks as though you had a grip on yourself. You'll be fine."

There didn't seem to be anything more to say. "I'm going now, if it's all right with you," Fex said. "I'm taking off."

"Yes," Mr. Palinkas said. "I expect you are."

23

THE FUNERAL HOME LOOKED VERY GAY. BEHIND ITS lighted windows many shadows moved. Fex made himself small as he followed Audrey up the path, dragging his feet as if he were going to the dentist. I don't know what to say, he thought. I don't want to go. I'm afraid. But I've got to. I've got to pay my respects. What shall I say? I'm sorry. I feel bad. Angie was my friend. I'll miss her.

Any or all of these things were true.

Please accept my sympathy. Once he'd heard his grandmother say, "May God have mercy on her soul," when a friend of hers had died. Wasn't that God's job, to have mercy on people's souls? Angie was a good lady. A kind person. There were plenty of stinkers around. Why couldn't one of the stinkers have died instead of Angie?

Standing on the top step, Audrey turned to see if he was coming. The door was flung open. A man stood there, dressed in a shiny black suit that must once have belonged to someone much bigger, much fatter than he was.

"Ah," the man said, as if he'd been expecting them, "there you are." Fex fought the urge to run. "Come in," the man said. Briskly Audrey did as she was told. Fex had no choice. He followed.

In the room beyond, the crowd roared like a seashell. Fex took a deep breath. "Why don't I wait outside?" he said in a squeaky voice. As if he hadn't heard, the man in the too-big suit said, "You'll want to see her."

Fex's head felt funny, not entirely his. The back of his neck tingled. Perspiration ran down inside his underwear. Audrey had disappeared.

"I came with my friend. Her name is Audrey," he babbled. His voice sounded ridiculous even to his own ears.

An old lady came at him.

"She looks beautiful!" the old lady said. Who did she mean? Audrey?

"Like a saint! Like a beautiful saint!" The old lady's little gray hand fell on Fex's shoulder. She gazed into his eyes, which were level with hers. The odor of fried fish clung to her clothes. He tried to work his way free. The smell of fish frying had always made him feel sick. She hung on. He wanted very much to hand her a karate chop he'd been practicing for some time, but he didn't dare. Not here. She wouldn't let him go.

"She was a wonderful girl," the old woman hissed. The strong smell of fish rose again to his nostrils, settled somewhere in his stomach. "You're a friend of hers, eh?"

Fex nodded, conserving his strength. He struggled silently. The little gray hands held firm.

"Come with me," she said. Candles flickered; heat and the scent of flowers overpowered him. He let himself be led.

Up ahead was a casket. He knew what it was, although he'd never actually seen one in the flesh. Or whatever you called it. He'd seen a picture of one once in a magazine. You've seen one casket you've seen them all, he thought. It was shiny, very shiny. Brand-new.

"There." The old woman's hands dug into him. Her voice was thin and triumphant. "Didn't I tell you? Is she beautiful or is she beautiful?"

She pushed him down, forced him to kneel beside the casket. It crossed his mind that she was extraordinarily strong for such an old person. "Say a prayer," she commanded. Fex put down his head, closed his eyes, and tried to pray. His mind was blank, the way it sometimes went in class when he was called upon to answer a question. Even when he knew the answer perfectly well.

He moved his lips in an effort to fool her.

Behind him, people moved, murmuring sorrowfully. Using up the oxygen. When your oxygen supply was used up, you passed out. Hadn't they just studied oxygen in science? He was going to pass out.

Fex forced himself to raise his head. He brought his eyes to the level of the casket's edge. The person lying there had a smooth, pink, untroubled face. Her lips were rouged and slightly smiling, as if at a private joke. Her glasses were gone. She wore a dress covered with dots. The dots made spots in front of Fex's eyes. An enormous sense of relief came over him. Why, that's not Angie, he thought. He'd never seen this person before in his life. It was all a mistake. Angie's not dead. This is someone else.

He started to rise, to get to his feet. He was going to get out of here even if he had to knock the old woman down.

"Sorry," he said in a loud voice. "That's not Angie. You've got the wrong person." He took a step away from the stranger lying there, lying peacefully in a dress with white dots. If they didn't know that Angie never wore dresses, with or without white dots, then they should. That did it. That made him know for sure that this wasn't Angie.

"Sorry," he said again. It seemed to him that everything

swayed: the room, the people watching him with open mouths, the candle flames, the flowers. Everything swayed. There must be a storm coming.

"Catch him," he heard someone say. "Get him," and that was the end of it.

24

"YOU O.K., ?" AUDREY ASKED, PEERING ANXIOUSLY AT HIM.
They were sitting on a bench in the hall of the funeral
home. They were alone. Even the old lady had finally
gone. So had the man in the too-big suit. The floor shone
with a peculiar brilliance that made Fex's head hurt.

"What happened?" he said.

"You fainted."

"I did not."

Audrey shrugged. She looked worn out. "O.K. Call it
what you want. What do I care? You feel well enough to
walk home, or should I call your mother to come get us?"

"I'm fine." He struggled to his feet. "Let's go." He

wobbled out into the air. The damp wind felt good against his face.

"What the heck happened to you?" he asked irritably. "One minute you were there and the next—whoof! you were gone."

"I just went and sat down," Audrey said. "Against the wall. I sat there, and the next thing I knew you were kneeling down by the coffin and putting your head down."

"It was the old lady. She made me."

"Anyway," Audrey went on, "next thing I knew, you keeled over. Fainted, whatever it was you did. Everybody started rushing around, and I told them I was with you, and they brought you out into the hall, and I waited until you were fine." She looked at him. "Are you fine?" she said.

Fex held himself very still. If he moved, something inside him might come loose. "Did I throw up?" he asked. His mouth didn't feel or taste as if he had. He didn't have the sour smell of throw-up on him, but he wanted to be sure.

"No," she said. "You looked like you would, but you didn't."

He was relieved. That would've been the end. They walked in silence to the corner, where they waited for the light to change.

"I didn't know men fainted," Fex said. "I thought it was only women."

"Women faint, men pass out," Audrey told him.

He was too weak to argue.

"I don't think that was Angie," he said. "It sure didn't look like her. I think they made a mistake. Either that or we were paying our respects to the wrong person."

"It was her, all right."

"How can you be so sure?"

"I talked to her husband. And her son. I told them we were sorry. They said thank you for coming. Her husband said Angie was getting supper, and she said she didn't feel so hot, and she lay down, and when they went to wake her up, she was dead." Audrey spread her hands wide.

"Then where'd she get that dumb thing she had on?" Fex said angrily. "That dumb dress. She never wore anything that looked like that, not when we knew her, and you know it. She wouldn't be caught dead in a dress."

Audrey stepped back, away from him, her eyes wide. The enormity of what he'd said swept over both of them. They began to laugh. Their laughter grew louder, harsher, more frantic. It merged with tears. They cried standing on the sidewalk while the light changed from red to green and back again to red. They cried with their arms hanging at their sides. For a brief minute they clung together, hanging on each other's neck like exhausted swimmers who had finally touched bottom, safe at last.

Then, through his tears, Fex noticed that Audrey's neck

had a faint, spicy odor. Funny. He hadn't noticed that smell the last time he'd touched her neck. The only other time he'd touched her neck. That night on the sofa in her house. That unforgettable night. This was different.

Fex's nose started to run.

"You got a handkerchief?" he asked. Audrey rummaged through her pockets.

"No," she said. He used his sleeve. By now they'd stopped crying. They were too tired to cry. They stayed where they were a little longer. Then they turned, and Audrey's hand bumped against his. Fex took it and together they headed for home.

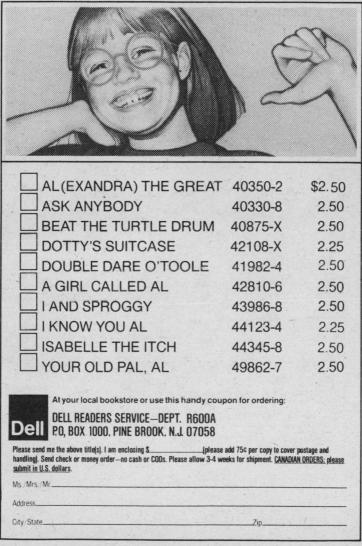

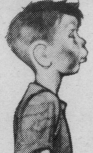

JudyBlume

knows about growing up. She has a knack for going right to the heart of even the most secret problems and feelings. You'll always find a friend in her books —like these, from YEARLING:

____	ARE YOU THERE, GOD? IT'S ME, MARGARET	$2.50	40419-3
____	BLUBBER	$2.75	40707-9
____	FRECKLE JUICE	$1.95	42813-0
____	IGGIE'S HOUSE	$2.50	44062-9
____	THE ONE IN THE MIDDLE IS THE GREEN KANGAROO	$1.95	46731-4
____	OTHERWISE KNOWN AS SHEILA THE GREAT	$2.50	46701-2
____	SUPERFUDGE	$2.75	48433-2
____	TALES OF A FOURTH GRADE NOTHING	$2.50	48474-X
____	THEN AGAIN, MAYBE I WON'T	$2.75	48659-9

YEARLING BOOKS

PATRICIA REILLY GIFF

writes about girls and boys just like you:

• clever   • cheerful   • stubborn

• mad   • brainy   • average

• happy

• sad

Show your parents this list of her funny, serious, wonderful books
—to own, read, and treasure for years!

_____ FOURTH GRADE CELEBRITY...........42676-6	$2.25
_____ GIFT OF THE PIRATE QUEEN 43046-1	2.25
_____ THE GIRL WHO KNEW IT ALL...........42855-6	2.50
_____ HAVE YOU SEEN	
HYACINTH MACAW?........................43450-5	2.50
_____ LEFT-HANDED SHORTSTOP............44672-4	2.25
_____ LORETTA P. SWEENY, WHERE	
ARE YOU? 44926-X	2.25
_____ THE WINTER WORM BUSINESS......49259-9	2.50

Yearling Books